WETWORK

Jones swung his knife in a savage stroke to open one man's throat as clean as a surgeon. Doc slammed his blade into one man's back as he kicked out with his right foot and sent the third bandit backward. As the man hit the ground, the two team members fell on him, burying their blades to the hilt in his chest.

Jones clamped his hand over the fallen bandit's mouth, jerked his head back and cut his throat.

It was all over in less than a minute.

Don't Miss the Next Exciting Thriller by
James N. Pruitt
Coming Soon from Avon Books

FIRE FORCE

LOBO ONE

JAMES N. PRUITT

AVON BOOKS  NEW YORK

LOBO ONE is an original publication of Avon Books. This work has never before appeared in book form. This work is a novel. Any similarity to actual persons or events is purely coincidental.

AVON BOOKS
A division of
The Hearst Corporation
1350 Avenue of the Americas
New York, New York 10019

Copyright © 1992 by Jim Pruitt
Published by arrangement with the author
Library of Congress Catalog Card Number: 91-93001
ISBN: 0-380-76616-7

First Avon Books Printing: February 1992

AVON TRADEMARK REG. U.S. PAT OFF. AND IN OTHER COUNTRIES, MARCA REGISTRADA, HECHO EN U.S.A.

Printed in the U.S.A.

RA 10 9 8 7 6 5 4 3 2 1

Chapter 1

The face of the Angolan scout was drawn tight. His large wide-set eyes darted left and right as they searched the shadowy darkness of the jungle that lined each side of the narrow trail. He ignored the increasing lines of perspiration that made their way down his cocoa-colored face and onto the sweat-drenched collar of his camouflage jungle fatigues.

Lifting his right foot carefully, he took a step forward. Assuring his right foot was firmly planted, he slowly and quietly brought the left foot forward. Pausing once again, he listened intently for the slightest sound. The men they were after were close—he could feel it.

The scout's gaze came to rest on a small pile of Savanna leaves to the right of the trail. Signaling for his squad to halt, he released the viselike grip on his AK-47 rifle and knelt down in front of the leaves. The nine men behind him stood motionless with their weapons poised. They strained their eyes and ears for any sound or the slightest movement from the dense jungle that now seemed to close in around them.

With the back of his hand, the scout wiped a drop of stinging sweat from his eyes before reaching down and brushing his fingers lightly over the spot that had drawn his attention. As he brought his fingers up to within inches of his face, a sadistic smile began to form at the corner of his mouth. Slowly he rubbed his thumb back and forth over his bloodstained fingertips.

The American-led guerrillas who had raided the compound this morning had extracted a deadly toll among the soldiers of the Angolan outpost. The attack had come at first light, a time when most men are not fully awake and so are unable to react. The attack was short, yet highly effective, lasting no more than ten minutes. As suddenly as it had begun, it was over. The guerrillas vanished back into the jungle.

The Cuban advisors and Angolan commanders quickly organized what remained of their shattered forces and set out in pursuit of the attackers. The order had been to capture if possible. It was an order that the scout knew would not be obeyed by him or the members of his squad. For just as the feeling of another man's blood slipping smoothly between his fingertips now ignited a strange lust within him, so it would be with his troops. It was a lust born of centuries of savagery. Cruelty, torture, and slow death were as much a part of this country as was the unmerciful rugged land itself.

The thought of capturing and torturing one of the Americans sent a rush of excitement through the scout. Standing up, he turned to face the members of his squad as he held his blood-smeared fingers high in the air. A smile crossed his face when he brought the fingertips to his lips and licked the crimson color clean.

Paul Stryker's first bullet caught the scout in the middle of the upper lip, sending most of the top row of teeth out of the back of the man's head. The second round struck him in the chin, tearing away what little remained of the man's face.

The action had been so sudden that it left the other members of the squad staring in disbelief at the headless body of their leader, who now lay crumpled on the ground. The scene froze them in place for only a second, but that was long enough. A hail of automatic weapons' fire tore through the Angolan unit. Screams of dying men mixed with the unending roar of gunfire and dull thud of bullets ripping through uniforms as they impacted on flesh and bone. In less than twenty seconds, it was all over. The only movement on the trail was the twitching of a hand or foot of one of the dead.

Paul Stryker emerged from the jungle and stepped onto the trail. His sweat-soaked fatigues clung to the broad shoulders and massive chest of his six-foot-four frame. His large hands held a Car-15 automatic rifle. Small whiffs of smoke still rose from its overheated barrel.

Moving cautiously among the bodies that littered the trail, he hooked the toe of his boot under one of the lifeless forms and flipped it over on its back. The front of the Angolan's shirt was a ragged, bloody mess. Icy, unmoving, coal-black eyes stared up at the blond man who had been his benefactor of death. It was a look Stryker had seen many times in his twenty-one years of military service. Even now, at age forty, he was still amazed at the look of surprise that accompanied the face of death. From the jungles of Vietnam, to Central America, and now to Africa, the faces always contained the elements of shock, confusion and the sudden realization that they had lost the ultimate game.

Cradling the Car-15 in the crook of his arm, Stryker pulled out a pack of cigarettes and lit one. The other three American members of the team moved out onto the trail and were followed by two squads of UNITA, African guerrillas. The taller of the three Americans began giving orders in Portuguese. He wanted the bodies searched, then moved off the trail. As the guerrillas began their task, the tall American walked in the direction of the mercenary leader.

Buck Buchanan was as big as Stryker. His short-cropped blond hair and soft blue eyes gave him the appearance of a small-town, all-American boy. Yet, he was forty, the same age as Stryker. Both men were ex-Green Berets who had met while working with the SOG groups in Vietnam. SOG was the shortened name of the Studies and Observations Group, which was later changed to Special Operations Group. It didn't matter what they called themselves; the missions were still the same— long-range recon across the borders of North Vietnam, Laos, and Cambodia.

Buchanan and Stryker had spent five long years running these high-risk missions together. In that time, they had been awarded every medal the Army had to offer except for the big one, the Congressional Medal of Honor. Many in Special Forces felt the infighting among the other services and a large dislike by those same people for Special Forces had played a major role in why the two men had not received their country's highest honor. It was a matter that had been blown off by Stryker and Buchanan. If they wanted to give it to them, fine. If they didn't—fuck 'em!

At the close of the Vietnam War, the two men

returned to Fort Bragg, North Carolina, the home of the Green Berets. Stryker was assigned to the Seventh Special Forces Group. Because he could speak Spanish, he soon headed to Panama and became involved in the hot little wars that were starting all over Central and South America. Buchanan went to the Fifth Special Forces Group, where he had the opportunity to see the Middle East up close. It had only seemed natural that they would join forces once more when they reached the twenty-year mark for retirement.

Stryker had been contacted by the CIA while on his last tour in El Salvador. They knew he was planning to retire and had offered him a job as a contract-filed operative and advisor. He had agreed to accept the job, but only if the Company would be willing to let him pick his own people to work with. The request had been granted. The day he returned to Fort Bragg, he found Buck and told him about the offer. Buck was quick to go along with him. After all, when you had spent twenty years jumping out of airplanes and fighting wars all over the world, it was hard to imagine yourself pumping gas or flipping burgers at Burger King.

Stryker pulled another cigarette from the pack and handed it to Buck. "The boy got a little careless, didn't he?" said Stryker as he flipped open a Zippo lighter and lit Buck's cigarette.

Buck glanced over at the headless body of the scout as he inhaled a deep puff off the cigarette. "Yeah. Kinda surprised me, too. He looked like the oldest of the bunch. You'd think he'd know better than to let them boys group up behind him like that."

Wiping the sweat from his face with the olive

drab rag that hung around his neck, Stryker said, "No shit! Too bad the Cuban instructor that he had wasn't with them."

Buck nodded in agreement as he asked, "How much time you figure we have before pickup?"

"Thirty, maybe forty-five minutes," said Stryker.

"I'll hustle the boys along. Won't want to miss our ride outta here," said Buck as he placed the cigarette in his mouth and turned to leave.

He had only gone a few steps when Stryker asked, "Buck, how's Sergeant Namba doing?"

Buck removed the cigarette from the corner of his mouth and slowly shook his head. "He didn't make it, Paul. Doc had him pretty well stabilized after he was hit this morning, but the damn holes opened up again while we were moving into position for the ambush."

Stryker's voice was low and held a marked sadness as he said, "Damn shame. Namba was one of our best men. It's not going to be easy telling his wife and family."

"I know, Paul. I don't envy you that job," said Buck as he walked away.

Pete Merrill and Chris "Doc" Shannon came over to Stryker. Both men were in their early thirties. Pete Merrill was one of the sharpest weapons specialists Stryker had seen come out of the Special Forces School in a long time. There were few, if any, weapons that he couldn't fire, teach, or rebuild from scratch. He was just as effective with the heavy 4.2- and 81-mm mortars.

Doc Shannon looked more like a teenager than a man thirty-two years of age. His light blond hair and deep blue eyes stood out against his tanned face. He might have lost Sergeant Namba today, but for every man that had been lost since they had been in Africa, Shannon had saved ten. Stryker had seen the medic perform surgery under some of the most primitive conditions. He could be working in any major hospital in the States, but the medic preferred the action.

Both Merrill and Shannon had left the Army after thirteen years. They had found the daily routine of peacetime Army life boring and not to their liking. Stryker had recruited them on one of his trips back to Fort Bragg.

The mercenary leader could see the self-accusing look in Shannon's eyes as he spoke. The loss of Sergeant Namba weighed heavily on the man.

"Paul, I'm sorry about Sergeant Namba. All that damn bouncing around on the litter while we were moving got him bleeding again. I just couldn't get it stopped. If only I hadn't had to move him and could have brought in a medevac we could . . . we could have—"

Stryker interrupted the medic as he placed his hand on the man's shoulder. "Hey, Chris, we know you did all you could. I'm sure Namba knew that, too."

"Jesus, man, he was hit four times, Doc. I don't know how you kept him together as long as you did," said Merrill.

Shannon knew the words wouldn't change anything, but at least they helped.

"Thanks, Paul, guess I just needed to hear that."

"Anytime, Doc," said Stryker.

Merrill waved his squad forward as he turned to Stryker and said, "Paul, I'm going to take the

squad and head for the LZ. We should have it secured by the time you arrive with the rest of the
teams.''

''Okay, Pete, watch your ass. You can bet they've
got spotter planes and choppers searching for us.
So far we've been pretty damn lucky. The Zaire
border is less than a mile away and I don't want to
lose anybody else.''

''I'm with you, boss,'' said Merrill as he waved
his point man forward.

''Later, man,'' said Shannon as the remainder
of the squad fell in behind Merrill, and the group
moved off the trail and faded into the jungle.

Double-checking to assure that all signs of their
presence and the deadly action which had occurred
here had been hidden, Stryker and the rest of the
attack group moved out in the direction of the LZ,
the landing zone. Stryker's force had parachuted
into Angola less than twenty-four hours ago, but
for the weary raiders, it seemed a lot longer than
that.

Pausing at the edge of the treeline that ringed
the LZ, Stryker keyed the mike on his radio and
whispered, ''Red Rover Three, this is Red Rover
One. How we looking? Over.''

Merrill's voice was low as he answered, ''Rover
One, Rover Three. We've completed a sweep of
the A.O.—everything is copesetic, boss. You have
a green light, over.''

''Roger, copy, Three. You will hold your position and provide cover fire for the first two birds
taking us out. Keep your people in the treeline until the third chopper touches down, then go like

hell. We'll cover from the air. You copy, Three? Over.''

"Roger, Rover One. Good copy. Standing by. Rover Three, out.''

Stryker cast a knowing glance in Buck's direction. Both combat vets knew that more often than not, what appeared to be a cold LZ could go hot in a matter of seconds. If they were going to be in a shoot-out with the bad guys, it was better to have it on the ground. At least there they could maneuver and had the option of attacking or retreating. Once they were in those choppers, their options were limited to only two directions—either up and away, or down and dead. His first chopper insertion onto a hot LZ in Vietnam had left Stryker with a better understanding of how a duck must feel with a hundred shotguns pointed at its ass. A hot LZ was anything but a pleasant experience.

The booming of an unfamiliar voice screaming over the radio startled Stryker. Grabbing the volume-control knob of his radio, he turned it down.

The chopper jockey sounded as if he was yelling into his mike. "Red Rover One, Red Rover One. This is Eagle Claw One, Eagle Claw One.''

Buck crawled over to Stryker's side. "Jesus! You believe this guy?''

Stryker managed a grin as he replied, "Hell, Buck, give the guy a break. He probably has a thing about LZs, too.''

Pressing his mike switch, Stryker spoke in a calm, low whisper. "Eagle Claw One, this is Red Rover One. No need to scream, sonny. We can hear you just fine, and so can everyone in the damn area, so let's take it easy, okay? Over.''

There was a momentary pause before the pilot came back on the air. This time the voice was lower, but Stryker could still hear the nervous edge in the words. "Roger, Rover One. Sorry about that. Guess we're just a little nervous. These Angolans have MIG-21s and they use Cuban pilots. So we've got a little of a pucker factor problem up here. Are we still on for the primary LZ? Over."

"Roger, Eagle One. That pucker factor's a condition we can relate to. You have a green light on the primary at this time. Sounds like you are about a mile out from our two o'clock. We do not have visual. Over."

"Good copy, Rover One. We are just beyond the ridge to your east, passing checkpoint three at this time. Have your people ready. We should be putting our feet in the water in about zero two. Eagle One, out."

With a short laugh, Stryker shook his head slowly back and forth. Buck looked over at his team leader and asked, "What's so funny?"

"Oh, nothing, man. That jockey's crack about putting his feet in the water made me think of a duck I once knew."

"A what?" asked Buck.

"Never mind, partner. Just a little self-induced, sick humor. That's all."

Buchanan started to say something, then let it go.

The whopping sounds of the rotor blades grew louder as the three Eagles suddenly appeared over the ridge. Two of them swooped in low and fast for the small opening of the LZ. The third chopper climbed to provide cover fire with its rockets and door-mounted mini-guns.

"Get 'em ready, Buck," yelled Stryker.

Buck went down the line, positioning himself behind his squad and Shannon's. Stryker could feel the increasing tension gripping his stomach as he watched the two birds throttle back. The tails of the choppers flared downward as the pilots lowered the skids to the ground among the blowing, whirling leaves and tall grass.

Stryker pointed to Buck, then waved in the direction of the choppers. Buck slapped Doc Shannon on the back as he yelled, "Go! Go! Go!"

Both squads leaped to their feet and broke from the treeline at a dead run, making their way through the shoulder-high elephant grass to the helicopters. Stryker waited until they were halfway to the birds before getting to his feet. He was about to break out into the open area himself when he caught a sudden movement out of the corner of his eye. To the left, five Angolan regulars were rushing through the trees, raising their rifles to fire on the teams and the choppers. Stryker cussed under his breath, "Goddamnit, I knew this was going too fucking smooth."

The five Angolans were so intent on reaching the edge of the treeline that they hadn't noticed Stryker jump back behind a tree. Semiautomatic fire was more accurate, but he needed to draw the attention of the five men and do it before they had a chance to open up on the choppers. Stepping out from behind the tree, Stryker positioned the muzzle of his Car-15 a few feet ahead of the advancing Angolans to compensate for the raising effect that would occur from thirty rounds being fired in a matter of seconds; he pressed his left hand down on top of the weapon to maintain as much control as possible. He pulled the trigger.

The sharp crack of the exploding rounds echoed through the trees like a runaway jackhammer. The outside man running to the left of the group was caught by two rounds in the leg and one in the groin. The deadly rain of bullets tore through the air like a water hose out of control. Stryker fought to keep the rifle down. Two more bullets hit the middle man in the shoulder and spun him sideways. A third bullet ricocheted off the side of a tree, striking the same man in the middle of the back and slamming him to the ground. Stryker swung the rifle back to the right just as he saw the glowing red tracer rounds ripping through the trees. The tracer rounds were a signal that his magazine was empty. The remaining three Angolans dove for cover as the tracers went over their heads.

Stryker leaped back behind the cover of the broad-based Savanna tree, released the empty magazine and rapidly inserted another full one. He could feel the heat from the barrel of the rifle through the open vents beneath the handguards. The radio hanging from his web gear was alive with traffic. Reaching for the mike, he pressed himself closer to the tree as a hail of bullets from the Angolans' AK-47s slammed into the branches and tore at the base of the tree.

"Rover One, Eagle One! Should we pull out?" The chopper pilot was screaming again.

Merrill broke in at the end of the pilot's frantic question. "Rover One, Rover Three. Hang in there, boss! We saw 'em and are closing in. Three out."

The pilot came up again. There was ever-increasing panic in his voice. "Rover One, how many are there? Oh, hell! We're gettin' the fuck out of here. You people call us when you have this LZ secured. Out.''

Buchanan, Shannon, and the two teams had hit the ground at the first sound of gunfire. They were now lying flat in the tall grass, still thirty yards from the choppers. Buck's voice was calm but threatening as he spoke into his radio. ''Eagle One, this is Rover Two. You lift those skids off the ground before I've got these people on board, and I promise you I'll shoot your fuckin' ass outta the sky my goddamn self. You copy that, asshole?''

Eagle One had already lifted the skids ten feet into the air when Buck finished his transmission. Now the UH1H helicopter lowered itself back down and settled on the ground.

''Uh . . . Two, this is Eagle. . . . We . . . we understand, but you guys got to get moving, man. . . . We're already picking up some Spanish transmissions on the other frequencies. Those damn MIG-21s could be here any minute.''

''Get 'em on their feet and into those choppers, Buck. That's an order!'' yelled Stryker.

''Roger, boss, we're outta here,'' came the reply.

Stryker watched across the open LZ as the squad leaders got their people on their feet and scrambling for the helicopters. Call signs and procedures went out the window as Stryker keyed his mike once more. ''Pete, I had five targets at eleven o'clock. Two are down hard. We've still got three out there somewhere.''

''Got it, Paul. We're moving in on your position now. We'll try to flush them out in your direction.''

"Rover One, this is Eagle Three. Do you want a gun run down there? Over."

Eagle Three was the cover chopper with the mini-guns and rockets that was circling high above the LZ.

"Negative! Negative, Eagle Three. We can handle it," replied Stryker. The last thing he needed right now was a chopper cutting loose with 6,000 rounds into the trees with good guys as well as bad guys moving all around the place. That was just asking for trouble and he had quite enough already, thank you.

Stryker edged himself to the right of the tree and peered around at the area where he had last seen the Angolans go for cover. The bodies of the two he had hit were still lying where they had fallen, but where in the hell were the other three? He was sure they had moved while he was reloading, but where?

A single shot rang out as splinters of bark flew from the tree inches from his face. Stryker rubbed at his eyes in an effort to remove the small pieces of wood that had momentarily blinded him.

Merrill was on the radio again. This time he spoke in a whispered tone. "Paul, we've got a fix on them. Hold fast and keep your head down. We're going to use grenades. They're between us, and I don't want to take a chance on firing on you, too. Let me know when you're ready."

Stryker watched as Eagles One and Two lifted off with the two teams as he said, "Go for it, Pete."

"Roger! Cover up. They're in the air."

Stryker forced his body in tight against the tree as three deafening explosions rocked the jungle.

Flying rock, dirt, and shrapnel tore through the air, some slamming into the tree he was behind, the remainder screaming past him and mutilating the trees beyond. Counting to three, Stryker rolled out from behind his cover and stared into the clouds of dusty gray smoke billowing into the jungle canopy. One of the Angolans came stumbling out of the smoke. His clothes were ripped and covered with blood. He still held his AK in one hand. The other hand was a shattered mess. Seeing Stryker, the man made a desperate attempt to raise the heavy rifle and fire, knowing that he would never make it. Stryker fired. Three shots hit the man in the chest, sending him backwards six feet. The rifle flew from his hand as he was knocked off his feet. He was dead before he hit the ground.

Merrill ran up to Stryker. "You okay, Paul?"

"Yeah. You done good, Pete. Get your people ready. We're getting the hell out of here before all this racket starts drawing a crowd."

Merrill nodded, then ran back to his team and began moving them toward the LZ.

Stryker called Eagle Three. "Eagle Three, get it on in here. We're clear and ready to head for the house."

"Roger, Rover One. Inbound ASAP. Out."

Stryker pulled a cigarette from the nearly empty pack. Placing it in the corner of his mouth, he lit it as he walked over to the bodies of the first two men he had killed when the action had started. They couldn't have been more than fifteen or sixteen years old. As he bent down and picked up the AK-47s, he couldn't help but wonder how much of a life these two kids could have had in fifteen years. It was a question that bothered him. Fighting men was one thing—but kids. It was something that he would never get used to. Too bad it didn't bother the people who had given them the guns.

Eagle Three touched down and the remainder of Stryker's force was loaded aboard and airborne within seconds. Leaning against the back of one of the pilots' seats, Stryker could feel the remaining surges of energy slowly drain from his body. The wind whipping through the open doors of the chopper against his sweaty jungle fatigues brought a welcome relief.

As he watched the green-and-brown-colored carpet of the jungle glide away below him, he tried to count the number of times he had taken this ride—a hundred, two hundred, a thousand. He couldn't remember anymore. It seemed a lifetime. His contract with the CIA was up in three months, and right now he wasn't sure if he was going to sign on for another eighteen months of this shit. He needed a break, some time to key himself down. More importantly, his mind needed a rest. Laying his head back against the vibrating pilot's seat, he closed his eyes. The faces of the two boys still lingered in his thoughts. Their bodies had been left on the jungle floor, but their faces had joined yet another army—Stryker's army of countless faces. It was an army that only marched in his nightmares.

Chapter 2

It was mid-April, and the North Carolina winter had lasted longer than normal. Paul Stryker and Buck Buchanan stood patiently at the luggage ramp of the Fayetteville airport waiting for their bags. Their dark tans drew an occasional glance from a few of the people waiting with them. Both men knew the more curious ones were playing a silent guessing game. Where were these two out-of-towners from? It had to be the West Coast or possibly Florida. There was no way they could have received those tans on the beaches of Carolina with the weather being as bad as it had been.

Buck leaned over to Stryker and whispered, "Boy, wouldn't these folks just shit if they knew we got these tans fighting Cubans in Angola."

Stryker kept his voice low as he answered, "I'm not so sure, Buck. Remember, this is Fort Bragg country. Besides the Green Berets, you've got the 82nd Airborne Division and the Delta Force. There's a lot of shit that goes on out of here. Most of it makes the national news. It may not shock as many of these folks as you think."

"You got a point there, Paul."

Grabbing their suitcases, they came down the ramp, went outside and hailed a cab for downtown

Fayetteville. As they pulled away from the curb, Stryker glanced out the back window at the massive construction that was going on around the airport.

"You know, I can remember when this place wasn't one half this size. Hell, there used to be cows roaming around where part of that runway is now. We had to fly those old prop jobs of Piedmont Airlines just to get to this place. Man, they've sure come a long ways since then."

"You said it, brother. Makes a guy realize how old he's gettin', don't it? But then, like they say, everything changes," said Buck.

"Well, that's one thing I hope I never see change."

Stryker was pointing to a road that led back into the pines. The street sign read DOC BENNETT ROAD. Below that and to the left was another sign with a large red arrow that read SPECIAL FORCES ASSOCI-ATION. Both of these men had spent more than their share of time in that clubhouse in the pines. Anyone who had spent any time at all in Special Forces knew where this club was located.

"Amen," said Buck. "I plan to retire on one of those big ol' comfortable bar stools when I get too old to run all over the world with my shootin' irons."

Stryker laughed as he asked, "And just when do you think that will be?"

"Oh, I'd say about the time I lose all my teeth, my hair starts falling out and I can't get my dick hard anymore."

Stryker stared at his running partner. A serious look came over his face before he said, "Jesus,

Buck! You mean this poor cabdriver is going to have to bring you back out here in the morning!''

''Fuck you, Stryker!''

Even the taxi driver was laughing as they swung out onto the main highway and headed for the Heart of Fayetteville Hotel.

Stryker and the other members of the team hadn't had to worry about renewing their contracts with the agency. One week after their raid into Angola, the CIA got the word from Congress that all aid to the National Unit for the Total Independence of Angola, better known as UNITA, had been cut off until further notice. Everyone, especially Stryker, had been a little more than pissed about the decision, but it was one that had not surprised a lot of people. Stryker had seen firsthand the ''on again, off again'' policies when he had worked with the Contras in Central America. The Iran-Contra hearings and the fact that it was an election year had played major roles in the congressional decision.

The Contras had been left to face a standing army of 600,000 in Nicaragua, while UNITA was left to take on the 30,000 or so Cuban, Russian, and East German advisors who were leading a modern army of over 60,000 Communist Africans.

Someone in the Agency had said that it was just the way of the world. Stryker knew better—it was the way of the politician. After the elections, the same assholes who cut off the money, knowing that their jobs were secure, would want to renew the aid to those heroic freedom fighters in Angola and Central America. They would be willing to dump millions of dollars and tons of weapons into the fight against Communist aggression. The only thing wrong with that kind of ideology was the fact that you had to have somebody from those groups still alive to give the money and guns to. Right now, if you looked at the odds, the Contras and UNITA were going to be hard-pressed to hold their own until after the elections. Only time would tell.

Arriving at the hotel, Buck paid the driver and took care of the bags while Stryker went inside to register for four rooms. Pete and Doc had gone home to visit their folks for a few days and were due in Fayetteville later that night. The Special Forces convention was being held in Fayetteville this year. Hotel and motel rooms would fill up fast as Special Forces people, both retired and still serving, began arriving from all parts of the world for the annual affair.

Stryker and the team had been offered another contract deal in the Middle East. After a team discussion, they all agreed to pass on the deal. It was time for a break. They had enough money to get by for the next six months, and the fact that the convention was going on at the same time was an added bonus. It would give them a chance to relax and see old friends. Stryker's team had proven themselves on more than a few occasions. They wouldn't have a hard time finding another contract when they were ready to go back to work unless the world had a sudden outbreak of brotherly love—and that didn't seem likely.

Stryker came out of the hotel office. Tossing Buck a room key, he said, "When you get your shit squared away, meet me at the Rustic."

"Got it," said Buck as he picked up his bags and headed for his room.

Stryker didn't bother unpacking. Throwing the bags on the bed, he left the room and made his

way around the pool to an adjoining parking lot.
Three cars sat in front of the club. The place still
looked the way he remembered it. They called it
the Rustic, and the name fit. It had been here as
long as Special Forces had been at Fort Bragg.
During the heydays of Vietnam, it had been the
primary watering hole for the Green Berets in
training, as well as a required stopover point for
the SF guys coming back from the mystical lands
of Southeast Asia.

The redwood building was shaded by a large oak
tree at the side and two more in the back. Black
wrought-iron railings lined the steps that led to the
entrance. The sign on the door read PRIVATE CLUB,
MEMBERS ONLY. Stryker tried to remember the last
time he had bought a membership card for the
place. Not that it really mattered. That membership business was no more than a formality that
protected the club owners from the alcohol-control
boys.

For all its growing and modernization, the city
of Fayetteville had yet to pass a liquor-by-the-drink
law, which could be attributed to the strong Baptist
influence in this part of the Bible Belt. If you
wanted the hard stuff, you had to bring your own
bottle. The bar girl would put a label on it with
your name, and you and the club were then legal.
If you happened to empty your bottle, there always
seemed to be another of the same kind that be-
longed to a Mr. Jones or Mr. Smith. The bar would
then assure you that your fellow club member
would have no objection to your having a drink
from his bottle. The state boys, of course, were
always trying to catch the club's owners selling
mixed drinks to non-club members or pushing il-

legal bottles. It was a game the two factions had been playing for years.

Entering the club, Stryker paused by the pool table to allow his eyes to adjust to the change from bright sunlight to the darkness of the interior of the room.

From somewhere on the upper level, by the bar, a familiar female voice yelled down to him, "Paul! Paul Stryker. You handsome son of a bitch."

Stryker's vision had focused by the time the long-haired blonde came from behind the bar and skipped down the three steps to the lower level of the club. Throwing her arms around his neck, she pressed her petite body into his and kissed him hard on the lips. He returned the kiss as he wrapped his big arms around her. Dropping his hands down to cup the firm cheeks of her rear end, he gave a playful squeeze. Breaking off the kiss but keeping her body pressed against him, she leaned back and stared lovingly up at him with her emerald eyes as she said, "Hey there, stud! You trying to get fresh with me?"

"Every chance I get, kid," said Stryker as he smiled down at her.

Lowering her head on his chest, she whispered in a low, soft voice, "Oh God, Paul, it's so good to see you again. Some bastard was in here a few weeks ago getting bombed out of his mind and said he'd heard you had been killed somewhere in Africa. It drove me crazy for a while. Then Sergeant Major McMullian came in one night and told me that it was bullshit. You were doing fine. I felt better then, but it still scared me, Paul."

Tightening his hold on her, he gently stroked her soft hair as he replied, "I think the old saying goes something like, 'The news of my death has been greatly exaggerated,' but it wasn't because they didn't try, honey.''

Kissing him lightly on the chin, she stepped back and pulled on his hand as she said, "Come on, Mr. Mark Twain, you look like you could use a Jack Daniel's on ice.''

Stryker followed her up the three steps to the upper bar. Patting her on the ass, he remarked, "I'm flattered that you remember.''

"Now that's a laugh. There are damn few women, if any, who could forget anything about you, Paul Stryker.''

Leaning back in one of the plush bar stools, he lit a cigarette and grinned. "Damn kid, you sure are great for an old man's ego.''

Sharon Boyer grinned as she set the drink in front of him.

"Hell, Stryker, you're not getting older; but damn, sugar, I don't know how you could possibly get any better.''

Leaving him with a sultry smile, she moved to the end of the bar and pulled two beers from the cooler for the only other customers in the place. Stryker sipped on his drink as he watched her bend over the cooler. The tight blue jeans strained every fiber as they clung to her perfectly rounded rear end. The sight stirred an urge within him. He had the sudden desire to leap over the bar and make love to her right there on the cooler. If it hadn't been for the two guys at the end of the bar, he would have seriously considered it. Sharon Boyer still had a hell of a body on her for a woman of forty-two.

Like most of the old-timers from Special Forces,

he had been coming to the Rustic off and on for the last twenty years. Charlie Boyer, a retired sergeant major from the 82nd Airborne Division, had owned the place for as long as Paul could remember. Contrary to popular belief, the members of SF and the 82nd who came to the Rustic got along well together. Arguments were settled on the pool table or with a game of bar dice, not fistfights and brawls. Those were reserved for the non-Airborne types who came in loud-mouthing and looking for trouble. The loyal patrons of the Rustic couldn't have found a man who held them in higher respect than Charlie Boyer. If the guys were broke, which in those days seemed to be all the time, Charlie would let them run a bar tab for the month and even loan them money if they were in a tight spot. In all that time, Stryker could not remember anyone who had not repaid Charlie for his kindness.

Stryker looked up at the small picture frame that hung beside the mirror behind Sharon. It brought back a fond memory. Rick Colby, a Special Forces recon man, had been killed in a firefight outside Da Nang in 1969. When the survival officer had conducted an inventory of his personal belongings for shipment back to the States, he found a handwritten will. Attached to the paper was a hundred-dollar bill. The money was to be sent to Charlie Boyer at the Rustic Lounge. Colby's orders for Vietnam had been a rushed affair, and he had forgotten to pay Charlie back the fifty dollars he had borrowed earlier. The extra fifty was for any other Green Beret who might be down on his luck. The money had arrived at the club the same day Rick Colby's name had appeared in the *Army Times* as one of the many killed in action that month. Charlie had been so touched by the will that he framed the hundred-dollar bill and hung it above a sign that read SPECIAL FORCES—A SPECIAL BREED OF MAN.

Raising his glass in a toast to Colby, Stryker finished the drink and watched as Sharon joked with the two customers at the end of the bar. She was like that, always having time to treat people nice. He had met her after his first tour of Vietnam. She had been home on spring break from the University of North Carolina and was helping her dad run the club. From the first moment he had seen her, he had been totally stunned by her beauty. The five-foot-five blonde with the Tuesday Weld smile and knockout body was everything he'd ever wanted.

She, on the other hand, had not been overly impressed with Stryker, but that hadn't stopped him. He spent every free hour in the club gradually working the Stryker charm on the young college girl. Their relationship grew over the summer. When she returned to college, he drove up to see her every weekend and holiday. By the end of the year, they even talked of marriage. The idea met with Charlie's approval.

Prior to Christmas, Stryker received orders for a second tour in Vietnam. Sharon was devastated by the news and begged him not to go. Charlie even offered to call in a few outstanding favors he had in Washington to get him out of the assignment, but Stryker refused. That refusal doomed any chance of marriage as far as Sharon was concerned. At first she wrote him often, but as the months passed the letters became fewer and fewer until they stopped all together. By the end of his tour, one of the new guys arriving in Vietnam told him she had married a football player at college and moved to Florida. Stryker extended his tour another six months. Buck said it this morning at the airport: things change.

Over the last fifteen years, they surely had. Charlie died of a heart attack and left the club to Sharon. She married three times, the last husband running off with some bimbo nightclub dancer, leaving Sharon with two kids she was now putting through college. She was a strong-willed woman who had never learned the meaning of the word *quit*. Maybe that was what drew him to her.

Stryker considered himself a lucky man. He had always seemed to return from his overseas adventures just when Sharon was between husbands. Each time he did, they would get together and party the night away. They would talk about Charlie, her kids or the old days. By morning, they would be in bed making wild, passionate love throughout the day. To some people, it might seem a strange relationship, but for them it was the only one that would work. She had given up on the idea of tying him down long ago. He was an adventurer, a shaker and a mover. He needed the battles and the action. She realized that now and was content to be with him whenever he was back—loving every precious minute of whatever time they had.

Coming back down the bar, she stopped in front of him and leaned forward to rest her small hands on his. "So, how much time do we have, Paul?"

Enjoying the softness of her touch on the backs of his hands, he smiled as he said, "Don't know, Sharon. Business is kind of slow. Could be months."

She could barely contain the excitement in her voice as she straightened up and gave out with a little-girl squeal and a beaming smile.

"Oh, Paul, that's wonderful! We can do so many things together. This god-awful weather is finally getting back to normal. Oh, this is fantastic! We can go to the beach, swim, cook out, and party our heads off like we used to."

Leaning forward, she glanced at the two men at the far end of the bar, then back at him. Undoing the top two buttons of her blouse, she leaned forward even more, giving him a perfect view of her small but firm breasts. With a wicked smile, she whispered, "We can lie on the beach in the dark, and we can do all those perverted sexual type things you've taught me over the years—you dirty old man."

The image of her lying naked beside him with the ocean waves breaking over the reefs sparked a longing within him like none he had known since the last time he had held her in his arms. He wanted her, and he needed her right now. Pure animal lust was in his steel-gray eyes as he spoke. "God, you drive me crazy—Sharon, close up early. Let's get out of here. I already have my room. We can be there in one minute and in bed in two. What d'you say, kid? Can you handle an afternoon workout?"

He could tell by the look of desire that spread over her lovely face that he didn't have to ask that question. Her eyes sparkled for a fleeting second, but then faded as she answered disappointingly, "Oh, Paul, you know I'd love to, but I can't. The health inspectors are coming at one and the state license people at two-thirty. I have to be here. I'm sorry, darling, really I am."

Sliding her warm hand up his arm, she continued, "If there was any other way, you know I would. You know how much I lov—" She cut the statement short of saying the word. Her emerald eyes pleaded for understanding.

Stryker did not disappoint her. Placing his big hands over hers, he flashed a grin as he said, "Hey kid, I understand. Hell, after all this time, I think I can suppress that raging snake I've got in my pocket for a few more hours."

She was smiling again as one of the customers called for another beer. Reluctantly releasing Stryker's hand, she started to walk away when he asked, "Do me a favor, okay? Point that pretty little ass of yours in the other direction when you bend over that cooler."

She giggled. "What's the matter, Green Beret? Can't handle the pressure?"

Before he could answer, the front door opened. Sunlight streaked past the large frame of Buck Buchanan as he stood in the doorway. His massive voice boomed around the room as he yelled, "Okay, motherfuckers! Drop your cocks and grab your socks. Big Buck's back in town."

Sharon turned to Stryker.

"This is just like old home week. You didn't tell me Buck was with you."

Stryker shrugged his shoulders. Buck moved up to the bar and slid onto the stool next to Stryker as Sharon asked, "Whiskey and Coke, Buck?"

"You got it, sweet thing. Damn, Sharon, you're lookin' good."

"So I've heard," she said as she made an exaggerated move to assure that her rear end was pointing straight at Stryker. She gave it a little wiggle as she bent over the cooler.

"That's one sadistic bitch," muttered Stryker.

"Yeah, but that's one fine-looking pair of blue jeans, brother. Mr. Levi would be proud."

Stryker nodded in agreement as Buck lit a cigarette before saying, "Paul, I called the airlines before coming over. Chris and Pete will be coming in on the eighteen-thirty flight tonight."

"No problem. I'll borrow Sharon's car, and we'll go out and pick them up. I've already got their rooms laid on."

Placing Buck's drink in front of him, Sharon leaned over the bar and gave the big man a kiss on the cheek.

"It's good to see you again, Buck."

"Thanks, sugar, you be sure and let me know when you're tired of hanging around with this slug and ready to go out with a guy with some class, okay?"

"I'll keep it in mind. You can count on it," she said as she winked at him.

Stryker slid his glass across the bar.

"Promises, promises. Give me another drink, you teasing Jezebel."

"Fuck you, Paul Stryker!" she replied.

"I certainly hope so," he said with a smile.

While Sharon fixed another drink for both men, Buck turned to face Stryker.

"You'll never guess who's registered in the room next to you."

"Okay, you got me. Who?"

"None other than our old team sergeant, Jake McKenna."

Stryker sat upright on his bar stool. "Jesus, Jake's here."

"You've got it. Saw the card in the office. I left a message with the desk. Told him we'd be at the Rustic."

When Sharon brought the drinks, Stryker asked, "Sharon, has Jake McKenna been here?"

"No, Paul, I would have told you. I didn't even know he was in town."

"Sure is," said Buck. "Checked in yesterday. I'm surprised he didn't come straight over here to see you, Sharon. Jake and your old man were pretty close."

Stryker noticed the look of concern that came over Sharon's face.

"What is it, Sharon? Is it something to do with Jake?"

"I'm not really sure, Paul. I've heard some pretty wild stories lately. Like you being killed in Africa. It's really hard to know what to believe anymore."

Both men directed their full attention to the pretty blonde as Stryker asked, "Come on, baby, what have you heard about Jake?"

"Well, you know when Jake retired, he took Charlotte and the kids and moved to Florida. He had a job with the Dade County Sheriff's Department, but you guys already knew that, didn't you?"

Both men nodded, with Buck adding, "Sure, Paul even offered Jake a job with us before he left, but Jake turned it down. Said he'd had enough of the Rambo shit. Like workin' for the law in Dade County was gonna be a picnic."

"Go on, Sharon," said Stryker.

"You remember Larry Wheeler, the weapons guy from the Fifth Group?"

Both men nodded again. "Yeah. He got out and went to work for the Drug Enforcement Agency," said Stryker.

"That's him. Well, he came in here about five months ago, and we were talking about people we knew when Jake's name came up. Larry had been working a case in Florida when Jake moved down there. He said Jake had had a hard time adjusting to the way civilians did things. He got into it with his bosses right after he got there. It was tough on Jake, but he knew he had to have the job, so he just kept his mouth shut and went on with business. Larry said he started drinking a lot. I guess it got pretty bad because Charlotte called Larry a couple of times to come out to the house and try to calm him down when he drank too much. It didn't help. Jake kept hitting the bottle nearly every night just to forget the job. It finally got out of hand. Larry wasn't sure what had happened, but it must have been more than Charlotte could put up with, because she took the kids and went back to Oklahoma."

Stryker shook his head as he said, "Damn. It had to be something awfully bad for her to leave him. They've been together for twenty years."

Sharon continued, "Larry said Jake went straight downhill after that. Started staying out all night. Showing up late for work and looking burnt-out when he did. It just seemed like nobody really gave a damn."

Buck growled, "Fuckin' civilians ain't got no time to help anybody. They got their own problems. It ain't nothin' like Special Forces, where guys watch out for each other. It's a hell of an adjustment; that's for sure. Didn't anybody notice how fucked up Jake was gettin'?''

Sharon rubbed the back of Stryker's hand as she answered, ''Oh, they reprimanded him a couple of times, but that was it.''

''Reprimand! Jesus Christ. I can just see Jake McKenna standing in front of some know-nothing supervisor and getting his ass chewed. Hell, they're lucky Jake didn't kill somebody,'' said Stryker.

Sharon lowered her head and stared at the bar before saying, ''He did!''

The two men looked at each other, then back to Sharon. ''You can't be serious, Sharon.''

''I'm afraid I am, Paul. Just before Wheeler was transferred to the West Coast, Jake was involved in a shoot-out with some drug dealers.''

''Hell, honey, that's an everyday thing in Florida.''

''I know, Buck. But Jake had been drinking on the stakeout. When the deal went down, Jake chased two of the guys into an alley. He had them cornered, so they threw their guns down and raised their hands. From the follow-up reports that Wheeler read, Jake was supposedly so bombed that he started yelling all kinds of crap at these two guys. Telling them they weren't going to walk away from this one, and what scumbags they were for selling shit that poisoned kids. He made them pick up their guns, then told them he was going to kill them. If they wanted any kind of chance at all, they'd better use them.''

''Damn. Didn't anybody try to stop it?'' asked Stryker.

''Larry said everybody else had their hands full

with a shoot-out with the other guys. Two DEA men finally got to the alley, but Jake yelled for them to stay out of it. The report said it was like watching a film clip from that movie *Gunfight at the O.K. Corral*. The bad guys had their guns in their hands and were holding them down at their sides. Jake was holding his the same way. One of the DEA guys screamed at Jake to stop, but he wasn't listening. Next thing you know, Jake yells at the drug dealers to go for it. When they made their move, Jake killed them both.''

"What the hell's the problem? He gave them a chance and saved the government money at the same time," said Buck.

"That's not the point here, Buck. This isn't Vietnam or Laos, where you can just pull out a gun and start shooting whenever you want to. This is the United States. There are laws and a justice system. Granted they're in bad shape, maybe, but there are still rules that have to be followed. Besides, that alone wasn't what got Jake suspended from the force."

"Suspended," said Stryker, "for blowing away two damn drug dealers? I know the system's a little screwed up, but those assholes were obviously guilty as hell."

"I know, Paul. Wheeler said they could have worked around the quick-draw business; but after Jake dropped both of these guys, he walked over to the bodies and fired three more bullets into each one of them. By then, of course, practically everybody involved in the operation was in the alley and watched him do that."

Stryker shifted his weight on the bar stool as he

said, "Hell, Jake must have really been wired that night."

Sharon stared up at his steel-gray eyes, "Paul, I'm sorry. I know you and Jake are like brothers."

"Yeah, he taught me everything about this business. Saved my ass more than once in 'Nam. I sure hate to hear he's got trouble now. Did Larry say what they did with him?"

"He wasn't sure how things came out. He had to leave before it was all over. The last thing he heard was that Jake was suspended and placed in the county hospital for observation. The D.A. was considering filing murder charges. They must have decided that the publicity wasn't worth it or he wouldn't be here now."

Stryker sat back looking over at Buck.

"I don't know, partner, maybe we're all crazy. Here's Jake McKenna, a guy who holds the Congressional Medal of Honor and has spent five years in a place called Vietnam and another four in Laos. He's been shot up and blown up more times than people can count, and now a grateful nation locks him away in a nut ward while they consider putting him away because he fucked over the rights of a couple of creeps who push poison to schoolkids. It's un-fucking-believable."

Buck finished his drink and set the glass back on the bar before he answered. "Yeah, I hear you. They love us when they need us and are embarrassed as hell when they don't—hell of a deal, ain't it? Look, I figure Jake could use a little company right about now. What d'you say we go find him and try to cheer him up?"

Stryker glanced down at his watch, then at Sharon. It was after one, and the inspectors still hadn't shown. She knew what he was thinking. Patting his hand gently, she said, "Go on, Paul. If you find him, you bring him straight back here so I can chew him out for not coming to see me the minute he got into town."

Grinning, Stryker stood on the bar rail and leaned over to kiss her.

"Thanks, baby. We'll be back by four."

"No you don't, Paul Stryker! Don't make promises you know you can't keep. If you two do find Jake, it might be days before I see you again. So you two boys just take those cute little buns of yours out of here, and I'll see you when I see you, okay?"

Buck laughed as he stood up. "Brother, has this lady got your number."

"Screw you, Buchanan!" said Stryker.

"Uh oh! You hear that, Sharon? I've been worried about this guy ever since I saw him looking at earrings and panty hose the other day. Now we know. He's AC/DC."

Sharon and the two customers at the end of the bar were laughing as Buck and Stryker headed for the front door. Moving down the steps to the lower level of the bar, Buck asked, "Would you really do that?"

"Would I really do what?"

"Screw me!"

"You're sick, Buchanan. You really are. Fuck you."

Buck bent his wrist slightly and in a high-pitched voice said, "Be the best piece you ever had, sailor."

There was another outbreak of laughter from the bar as the door closed behind the two men.

Chapter 3

The radiant colors of red and orange reflected off the clouds as the sun settled slowly beyond the mountain ranges to the west of Na Pho.

Father Rogers finished his prayers. Making the sign of the cross, he rose to his feet and let his eyes take in the beauty of the mountains of Thailand at sunset. He had had reservations about this assignment at first. Na Pho was a refugee camp for displaced Laotians and Vietnamese who were still fleeing the rolling tide of communism which was sweeping Southeast Asia. The great world powers, who at one time had promised so much to these now desolate people, had lost interest in the region and abandoned the believers and followers to fend for themselves. For those Americans who fully understood what had happened in Southeast Asia, this abandonment would always be a national disgrace.

Father Rogers had tried to analyze the situation before his arrival. It was one that seemed more and more in line with the times. Presidents and dictators, backed by their congresses or political councils, instigated the wars. Generals and soldiers directed and fought them, and in the end, the only true losers were the people of the land, who had never really understood why it had all started anyway.

Within days of his arrival, Father Rogers had found conditions were far worse than he had been led to believe. The number of refugees had been underestimated by at least two thousand. Food supplies from the Thai government, the Red Cross and the United Nations were all exhausted within a matter of only a few days. The supply could not keep up with the demand. People of other countries had lost interest in the plight of Asians. The amount of food had steadily decreased as a busy world forgot the people of Na Pho and went on about its own business.

The priest found that he could only feed seventy percent of the people in this overcrowded camp. The younger children faced a slow death from starvation. Appeals to Rome and churches in the States went unanswered. The elderly had all but accepted their fate. What little food was provided them, they passed on to their children, until one night, in the grasp of old age and without hope, they quietly died in their sleep. It was a situation that truly tested the faith of the most avid believer. Yet, each evening, Father Rogers knelt by the chain-link fence and rows of razor-sharp barbed wire that surrounded this place of desolation and misery, and asked for guidance from the Almighty.

A major television network from the States had spent a few days in the compound, filming the living conditions of the people and conducting interviews. He had appealed to the world for assistance. After the show had aired around the world, via cable, Father Rogers had received thousands of letters of sympathy, but very little money. The day-to-day, hour-by-hour survival of so many of God's children weighed heavy on his mind as he now watched the sun slowly disappear beyond the mountains.

The soft voice and the gentle hand that touched his shoulder averted his thoughts from the darkness that had begun to fall over Thailand.

"Father, I am afraid the elder Mr. Qhuan is dying. His wife asked that you please be with them when the time comes."

The priest turned and stared into the beautiful blue eyes of Denise Randolph. The television special had not generated a lot of money, but it had touched the heart of this attractive young woman. She had arrived at a time when he had found himself questioning the Lord's reasons for so much suffering. The sisters had believed her arrival to be a good omen. A sign of hope. This was Denise Randolph, daughter of one of the richest men in the world. At first, Rogers had been concerned that the young jet-setter, who had never known a night's hunger, was simply here to play some silly little girl's game to impress her equally rich friends. His interrogation of her had been considered rather ruthless in the eyes of the sisters, but in the end, Denise had prevailed. Over the past two months, she had proven herself. She worked long hours with the sisters, as well as with the Laotian and Vietnamese camp leaders. No job was ever too large or too small. She had gained the respect of the entire camp for her efforts. She now repeated her statement.

"Father. I'm sorry, but Mrs. Qhuan asked that you please be with them when the time comes."

"Yes, of course. Thank you, Denise."

She nodded, then turned to walk away. He stopped her.

"Denise."

"Yes, Father."

"I just wanted you to know, we are all grateful to you for all you have done here. Your father must be very proud of you."

Looking away from him, she stared down at the ground. The young, well-built woman of twenty-three was slightly embarrassed as she answered, "No, Father, it is I who should be grateful. If I hadn't seen that television special, I would be on one of my father's jets right now flying to Paris or London with a group of my so-called friends. We'd all be getting drunk or high, not even knowing what day it is and caring even less. My friends think I'm crazy, and Daddy believes it's just a phase I'm going through. You know, the last time we were in town, I called him. His secretary told me I had five minutes because he had an important meeting he had to attend. I didn't even wait for her to transfer the call. I just hung up."

Rogers gave her a look of understanding as he said, "Regardless, my child, I am certain he is proud of your accomplishments and he is concerned for you; otherwise, he would not have sent those four security men from his company to watch over you while you are here."

Denise could not conceal the disappointment in her voice as she said, "Oh, I know he loves me, Father. I suppose I was hoping he would be concerned enough to come here himself, to finally tear himself away from that damn business long enough to be with me for a few days."

Denise noticed the sudden rise of Father Rogers's eyebrows as she said *damn*. "I'm sorry, Father, I guess I just got carried away."

A gentle smile crossed his kind and caring face as he took her hand and replied, "Don't worry about it, my child. Believe me, there are times that I have—in silence, of course—said or thought the same thing. We have so little and there are so many."

She squeezed his hand gently in her own. "You are doing all you can, Father. They all realize that, and for your efforts, these people bless you in their prayers every night."

"God bless you, my child," he said as he kissed her on the forehead. "You bring joy to an old man's heart. I must go now. Sister Maria may need your assistance with the bathing of the children tonight. Could you help her please?"

"Of course, Father."

She watched as he made his way across the compound and disappeared into the ramshackle structure of cardboard and tin that had become the home of the Qhuan family. Father Rogers was such a caring and kind man. If only her father understood her as well as this man did. She was a long way from the nightlife of Paris or Monte Carlo, but she was happier now than she had ever been in her life. For once she was doing something for someone besides herself, and she was doing it without her father's money or influence. That thought sent a warm feeling of accomplishment through her. If only her father could take the time to share this feeling with her, it would make her happiness complete.

* * *

By nine-thirty they had finished the baths. Dumping the tubs and folding the towels away, Denise and Sister Maria walked out into the warm night air. The sky was clear and dotted with thousands of twinkling stars. Maria was thirty-two years old and the youngest of the three nuns who had arrived with Father Rogers. She was from New York and had been with the order for six years. Denise liked the other sisters, but Maria was closer to her own age and they worked well together.

As they stopped at the fence, they both smiled and waved to the Thai guard who walked by as he made his rounds outside the wire.

"You got a cigarette, Denise?"

"Sure."

"Well hurry up and light the thing before the guard comes back around," said Maria in her gruff New York accent.

That was another reason Denise got along so well with Maria. She was one of the "new generation" nuns. She didn't wear a habit. Instead she wore blue jeans, tennis shoes, and an array of T-shirts that had "Property of the New York Jets" embossed across the front. The one she wore tonight was green with white letters, and it fit snugly over a very ample chest.

Passing the cigarette to Maria, Denise watched the woman inhale deeply then exhale, saying, "Oh, yeah, I've needed that for the last two hours. I started to sneak out earlier, but I couldn't bring myself to leave you with ten kids in the tubs."

Denise lit herself a cigarette as she said, "Thanks, I appreciate that. It's a beautiful night, isn't it?"

"Yes it is," answered Maria as she looked up

at the stars. "Wonder what they're doing in the old neighborhood in New York tonight?"

"What part of New York are you from, Maria?"

"One of those out-of-the-way places on the east side. Damn tough bunch of kids come outta there. You know, when I was fourteen, I use to have to beat the boys off." Placing her cigarette-free hand on one of her large breasts, she continued, "Early bloomer. Know what I mean? Use to drive them boys nuts. Every one of 'em was trying to get their hands on these so they could run back to the club-house and tell the rest of the guys how they'd copped a feel of the biggest pair in the neighbor-hood. You ever have that problem, Denise?"

Denise's hand unintentionally moved up to one of her small breasts. They were nowhere near the size of Maria's, but they could still draw a look from the boys. Maria smiled a wide smile at her.

"That's okay, honey. I'm sure you've had your share of gropers and squeezers. But let me tell ya', those New York boys used to grab and start twistin' and pulling like they were trying to adjust a damn radio knob. Hurt like hell, too. But I never let any of 'em go any farther than that. I wasn't about to get knocked up by one of those retards, no sir. I watched my poor mother try raising eight of us. Almost killed her in the long run."

Denise took another puff off her cigarette before getting up the courage to ask, "Maria, didn't you ever . . . I mean . . . haven't you ever . . . Oh! You know what I mean?"

"Oh goodness yes, darling. I haven't been a nun all my life. We had this really great-looking guy transfer from another school. I mean this guy was like a Greek god—blond hair, blue eyes and a bod that wouldn't quit. Every girl in the school flipped over this stud. I guess I didn't play fair. I used my God-given, radio aptitudes on the poor boy.'' Maria laughed as she cupped her size 38Ds and pushed them up and down a couple of times. ''Had that stud wrapped around my finger in no time. Needless to say, within a couple of weeks we were wrapped around each other in the back seat of his Daddy's car.''

Denise almost choked on her cigarette as she giggled. Maria was nothing like the nuns she had read or heard about; that was one of the reasons Denise liked her so much. She was honest and fun loving; however, in the two months she had been around the girl from New York, Denise had seen how dedicated the woman was to her work, even if she did have a tough-edged way of showing it.

''Did the subject of marriage ever come up, or did he just get what he wanted and then split like most of them do?''

Taking a long drag on the smoke, Maria saw the guard round the corner of the fence. Holding the smoke in, she nodded and blessed him as he strolled by. Once he was out of sight, she blew the smoke out as if it were nothing and said, ''No, nothing like that, Denise. As a matter of fact, I had spent so many years trying to save myself for the right guy that when that boy showed me what I'd been missing, I dumped him and started laying just about every boy in school. Had a hell of a good time, too.''

Denise couldn't contain the laugh that broke forth as she asked, ''My God, Maria, what ever made you become a nun?''

The tall, well-built brunette stared up at the sky

in silence for a moment before she answered. "Oh,
I kept messing around until one day I got pregnant.
Had a baby girl. Named her Maria Louise. That
was a name my grandmother had always wished
they had given me. The father could have been any
of ten guys, but that didn't matter. I really didn't
want a husband anyway. I mean, having a man
around once in a while was one thing, but Lord,
having to put up with one day and night forever
scared the hell out of me. I got a job, and little
Maria and I were doing fine. One night I went in
to check on her, and she . . . she wasn't breathing.
She was dead. They said it was crib death. Nobody
could explain what caused it. My mother told me
it was God's way of punishing me for my sins.
Guess it made me wake up to just where my life
was going, so here I am. I became a nun more out
of memory of Maria Louise."

Denise was sorry she had asked. "Maria, I . . .
I'm sorry. I didn't mean to bring up old painful
memories."

Flipping the cigarette butt through the fence, the
nun turned to Denise. "No need to apologize. I
lost a daughter, but God has forgiven me and provided me with hundreds of little girls to care for
now."

Tears were welling up in her eyes as Denise
reached out and hugged Maria. They wiped the
tears from each other's eyes. Holding hands, they
turned away from the fence and walked back toward their rooms. From somewhere in the darkness
of the compound the loud thud of an 81-mm mortar
firing reverberated through the night air. Seconds
later the sound was followed by a pop, as a round

of illumination lit up the sky and the area beyond the fence.

Maria had felt Denise's body tense when the round had been fired.

"Don't worry, Denise, they're just checking the perimeter."

Denise's hand was still trembling as she replied, "Oh, I know. One of Daddy's security people explained how the mortars work and why they fire them at night, but I'm never ready for it and it scares the hell out of me. You'd think after two months here I would—"

Before she could finish there was a rattle of gunfire from somewhere along the east wall. Maria clutched Denise's hand tightly and suddenly stopped walking. Her eyes turned in the direction of the gunfire. "What is it, Maria?"

Automatic weapons fire broke out all along the east wall. It was louder and more sustained this time. Maria released Denise's hand and yelled, "Run, Denise! Run for the church—get in there and do it now!"

All the mortars in the camp were firing now. The noise was deafening. Her voice tense with fear, Denise screamed, "My God, Maria. What is it? What is happening?"

"Damn it, Denise, just do what I told you. Get to the church and don't come out of there until Father Rogers or I come for you. Now hurry!"

Maria rushed off in the direction of the sisters' quarters. Denise still wasn't sure what was happening. Thai soldiers were dashing back and forth across the compound dressed in full combat gear and carrying all kinds of weapons. A look of fear and desperation outlined the shadows of their faces.

The loud sounds of the mortars were coming from everywhere. Some were still firing illumination, while others were hurling deadly explosive rounds outside the fence. The explosions lit up the sky and tossed huge chunks of earth and jungle foliage high into the air.

Suddenly, someone grabbed her around the waist. It was Keith Phillips, one of her father's security men. He clutched a rifle in his hand as he yelled, "Miss Randolph, hurry! We've got to get to cover. It's an attack!"

Confusion reined in her voice. "Under attack? What do you mean? They can't . . . This is Thailand, for God's sakes."

Grabbing her by the arm, Phillips began to pull her along behind him as he said, "We've got to hurry, Miss Randolph."

The ground shook as an incoming mortar round exploded in the center of the compound. Phillips threw her to the ground. Pieces of jagged metal and rock cut their way through the air above her head. She heard a dull thump somewhere above her, as she felt a heavy weight fall across her body. There were three more rapid explosions. The sound of gunfire reached a fevered pitch. For Denise, it was a nightmare of blinding flashes mixed with the screams and cries of children, hysterical women, and frightened men.

She struggled to pull herself to her feet, but the weight across her body pinned her firmly to the ground. Where was Phillips? Why wasn't he trying to help her? She forced herself onto her side. Her questions were suddenly answered. The loud pop of an illumination round directly above her lit up the area. In the dull yellow glow of the swinging light, she saw the lifeless body of Keith Phillips. His eyes were wide open and staring at her. A huge gaping hole at the right side of his neck was squirting streams of blood from the severed jugular vein. Blood covered her pants and spread like a pool in the dirt around her. She screamed hysterically for help.

A Thai soldier stopped in mid-stride a few yards from her. Rushing to her side, he pulled the body off her and reached down to help her to her feet. He had her halfway up when his body suddenly jerked. A look of surprise came over his face. He released his grip on her, and she tumbled back to the ground. The soldier stiffened upright as a small trickle of blood pushed its way through his lips at the corner of his mouth. The rifle slid from his hands as he took two steps, then fell forward. His head bounced once as it slammed into the dirt. Two large red circles began to spread in the middle of his back. The two bullet holes were less than one inch apart. The man was dead.

Denise screamed again. This couldn't be happening. She had to find Father Rogers. She felt faint. Her mind was confused. She couldn't think straight. Everything was happening so fast. Denise managed to pull herself to her feet and staggered half dazed in the direction of the church. To her right, she saw a Laotian mother carrying a baby in her arms and dragging a small girl behind her. They were trying to reach a ditch only a few yards away in order to find cover from the incoming rounds that were now falling like rain from the sky. They never made it. A blinding flash consumed them, and they were gone. Only a smoldering crater remained where they had been standing.

Denise's lungs felt as if they were on fire as she tried to stay on her feet. She was almost there. The church was only thirty yards away now. Tears streamed down her face as the same thought kept running through her mind: They're going to kill us. My God, they're going to kill us all. I'm going to die.

Twenty yards. More blinding flashes to her left and right. The increased sound of gunfire signaled that a full-scale battle was in progress, and the sounds were getting closer. Ten yards. . . . The doors of the church swung open. She saw Father Rogers outlined in the light from inside the church, reaching out his hand and yelling for her to hurry. A sense of relief spread over her confused mind as she reached out her own hand.

The small feeling of safety quickly vanished as her eyes widened in disbelief at what she saw.

The front of Father Rogers's shirt appeared to jump forward from his chest. Once, twice, then a third time. His outstretched hand fell motionless to his side. A bright crimson color covered the front of his shirt as he fell sideways in the door. A scream came from the very pit of Denise Randolph's stomach as she watched helplessly as the priest crumpled in the doorway, his body rolling haphazardly down the wooden steps and coming to rest in the dirt, only a few yards in front of her.

Dropping to her knees beside Father Rogers, she cradled his graying head in her lap. Her tears were flowing beyond control as she yelled, "Oh, God, why? Why this man? Why have you forsaken us?"

She felt the priest's hand touch hers as he tried to speak. Only blood came forth. With his remaining strength, he squeezed her small hand, and through the blood that now streamed from his nose and mouth, he managed to utter, "No . . . no, my child. . . . You . . . you must keep faith. . . . He will not . . . not forsake you . . . believe . . ." The words faded as he drew his last breath.

Denise sat, rocking him back and forth in her lap. Unable or unwilling to let go of the man she had come to love so much. The light from the doorway of the church shone down on his face as her trembling hands wiped the blood from around his nose and lips. Tears dropped into the gray hair of the head she now caressed ever so gently. Again she asked herself, "Why? Why this man, Lord?"

The question had no sooner passed her lips than a shadowy figure blocked the light pouring out from the doorway. Looking up, she saw the form of a man. He held a rifle pointing upward with the stock resting on his hip. A gravelly voice asked, "Is the priest dead, bitch?"

She stopped the rocking motion, stared up at the threatening voice, and struggled to control her emotions as she replied, "Yes, he has gone to meet his God."

The man on the steps responded to her words with a hideous laugh. "Is that so? Then I have done him a great service this night. I am sure they will both have much to talk about."

"Who . . . who are you?" she asked. "Why have you attacked these helpless people? Haven't they suffered enough? What is it you want here?"

Still laughing as he made his way down the steps, he stopped in front of her. With his free hand, he grabbed her by the hair. Jerking her head back, he leaned forward into her face. The foul odor of his breath brought her to the verge of nausea as he yelled, "I am Colonel Phon Van Bao. I need no reason to slaughter these worthless sheep. Many are cowards and deserters from my own country of Laos. Nor do I fear the Thai dogs that give them refuge. I go where I please, and I take what I want. And you—you American bitch! I want you. My men can have the sluts of this camp, but you . . . you shall be mine."

In a meek trembling voice she whispered, "Oh my God."

Savagely jerking her backwards by the hair, he threw her onto the body of Father Rogers. "There is your God, whore!" he screamed. "Why do you ask his help? He could not even help one of his own believers."

Once more the man broke into sickening laughter that sent a chill down her back. Looking away from the cause of her fear, she grasped the bloody hand of the dead priest, huddled her shaking body close to Father Rogers, and began to pray, "Our Father, who art in heaven, hallowed be thy name. Thy kingdom come, thy will be done . . ."

Colonel Bao turned away from her and yelled to one of his soldiers who had just come out of the church, "You! You will stay with this woman until I come for her. If she should escape, I shall split your worthless gut from head to toe. Do you understand?"

The ragged-looking soldier, dressed in a fatigue shirt and blue jeans, brought his AK-47 rifle up in front of him at attention to acknowledge Bao's orders.

The mortars had stopped, and now only a few sporadic rounds of gunfire could be heard around the compound. The army of Laotian bandits were running wild throughout the camp, kicking in the makeshift doors of the terrified refugees. They ransacked what few meager belongings they could find. Those who tried to resist were beaten down with rifle butts or simply shot outright.

Colonel Bao paused at the shattered door of one of the rooms and watched as four of his soldiers tore the clothes from a young girl who could have been no older than thirteen. Throwing her to the ground, three of them held her screaming, struggling body down while the fourth tore at his belt. Dropping his pants, he threw himself on top of her. There was a high-pitched scream of pain as he positioned himself over her; then he slammed forward with all his might. The girl's cries only excited her attacker more as he began rocking back and forth on top of her amid the cheers and laughter of those who held her small arms and legs pinned to the ground.

The mother of the girl sat huddled in a dark corner of the room, sobbing silently, her hands clasped tightly over her ears so as not to hear the screams of her only child. In another corner, her husband lay across a bamboo bed with a bullet hole in his forehead.

Bao lit a cigarette as he watched the rape. He thought of the pleasure that awaited him with the American girl with the yellow hair. One after another, the soldiers took the child. The third man pulled his sweaty body from her and was quickly replaced by the fourth and final man. There was no longer a need to hold her down. Tear-stained eyes stared aimlessly up at the ceiling. The young girl had accepted her fate.

Bao glanced at his watch. Twenty-five minutes

had passed since the attack began. Even with the destruction of the communications center at the outset of the battle, he knew it would not be long before the Thai army sent a unit to investigate. He had allowed forty-five minutes for the operation from start to finish. He would stay with that schedule. Flipping the cigarette to the ground, he spoke to the half-naked men around the girl, "Get this business over with! We are leaving."

Three of the men scrambled to their feet, pulling their pants up as the colonel walked away. The fourth soldier continued to push and grind himself into the motionless girl. One of the other men yelled down to him, "Come, Bien, we must go."

Turning his sweaty face up to the others around him, the man called Bien cried, "It is not fair! The three of you have ripped and torn her so bad that it is now like fucking a dead fish."

"No matter," said another, as he placed his jungle boot on Bien's buttocks and pushed him off the girl. "The colonel said we are leaving. So stop your complaining and come on."

The soldier was still cursing as he pulled on his pants and fastened his belt. The other three left the room as Bien picked up his rifle. Pausing a moment to look down at the tormented face of the ravaged girl, he spit on her small breasts. His eyes roamed down to the smeared blood between her legs.

"You could not even make a good whore now, you squealing little pig."

Stepping through the shattered doorway, he stopped, turned back to look at her once more and said, "If you could not make a good whore—then what good are you?"

Raising his rifle, he pointed it into uncaring eyes and pulled the trigger. The loud crack of the single bullet that blew half her face away echoed through the burning, smoke-filled camp. It was followed by the screams of a mother for her child. They were sounds these jungles of Southeast Asia had heard countless times before. . . .

Chapter 4

Early-morning sunlight streaked through the bent and broken window blinds of the hotel room as Jake McKenna pulled the perfume-scented pillow tight against his face. Across the room, he could hear the irritating voice of a woman giving the weather report for Fayetteville and the surrounding areas of North Carolina. God, he wished she'd shut the hell up. His head felt like it was going to come off at any minute, and the woman with the high-pitched voice wasn't making it any better.

No sooner had the weather lady finished than the phone next to the bed rang. It sounded like the bells of Saint Mary's were clanging around the room. Reluctantly pulling his face from the pillow, keeping his eyes closed, he rolled over and groped for the phone on the nightstand. A low moan made its way through the hangover as his fingers fumbled along the top of the table, knocking the receiver off the hook. Pulling the two-headed monster across the sheet by the cord, he brought it up to his mouth and uttered through dry, cracked lips, "Yeah . . . yeah! Who is it?"

A young woman's voice came back over the line. "David! Oh David, I'm sorry we had the fight. I really do love you. Please, don't leave. We can work this out. Really we can.''

McKenna forced his bloodshot eyes open as he asked, ''Who in the fuck is this?''

There came a long moment of silence and then, ''Who . . . who are you? You're not David.''

''No shit, lady!'' McKenna's head was pounding now. ''You got the wrong fuckin' number. No wonder the guy's leavin' your ass! You can't even dial a fucking phone right.''

Tossing the receiver off the bed, he rolled over, closed his eyes and tried to go back to sleep. After a few minutes he realized something was wrong. Gone was the sweet scent of the pillow. It had been replaced by a strong odor that somehow seemed familiar to him. Forcing his eyes open once more, he raised himself up on one elbow. The brightness of the room sent shock waves through his aching eyes and straight to his brain. God, he felt terrible.

He slowly turned his head to the right. What he saw made him feel even worse. Next to the pillow lay the scattered remains of a large pizza; a half-empty can of beer lay on its side surrounded by soaked cigarette butts. The beer had leaked out onto the bed. The sheets were wet. That wasn't too hard to take, but the small pile of vomit in the far corner of the box brought the ex-Green Beret out of the bed and sent him rushing for the bathroom.

After ten minutes with his head in the commode and another ten in the shower, he made his way out of the bathroom. He still wasn't feeling great, but at least now he didn't figure he was going to die.

Standing in front of the mirror, he stared at the dark circles under his eyes. Small red lines made their way in all directions from his light blue eyes. The forty-five-year-old man hardly recognized the unshaven leathery face staring back at him. Generally, he looked like hell.

It was not until he saw the demolished room reflected in the mirror that he realized he didn't know where he was. It sure as hell wasn't the Heart of Fayetteville Hotel. Looking down at the monogrammed towel that was wrapped around his waist, he read the words *Holiday Inn*. Staring back in the mirror, he asked the stranger he saw there, "Now what the hell are we doing at the Holiday Inn?"

His cigarettes and lighter were lying on the dresser by the lamp. Next to them lay his billfold.

"Oh shit!" he said as he picked up the wallet and opened it. He expected to find it empty. He was pleasantly surprised. The credit cards and money were still there.

"Easy now, old man. Get hold of yourself. Think about it for a minute. Where were you last night and just who the hell were you with?"

The effort was beginning to increase the pain in his pounding head. He had checked into "the Heart" early yesterday morning. He remembered heading straight for the Rustic, but knew he'd have to have a bottle if he wanted to drink the hard stuff. Of course. The liquor store, that was it. He'd met a tall good-looking brunette at the liquor store. What was her name? He burnt up a few more brain cells, but still couldn't remember her name. There was one thing he did remember—she had a hell of a body on her. He made small talk with her and cracked a few jokes that made her laugh. One thing led to another and by that afternoon they hit a few of the clubs and ended up at the Holiday Inn.

Lighting a cigarette, he walked over to the bed. A glance at the pizza box almost brought on another mad dash for the bathroom. Holding his breath, he removed the cardboard mess from the bed and placed it outside the door. Sitting on the edge of the bed, he looked down and found a half-empty bottle of Jack Daniel's at his feet. Picking it up, he unscrewed the cap as he studied the remains of the suite.

The coffee table lay on its side; one leg had been broken off and was sticking out of the wall above the headboard of the bed. An empty Jim Beam bottle lay by a chair with torn cushions. One of his cowboy boots was on top of the television—no telling where the other one was. His pants hung from the dresser with the cracked mirror, and his shirt was wadded up in the corner.

Staring down into the open bottle that he held tightly in his hands, he slowly shook his head back and forth. What the hell had happened in here? Jake honestly had no idea. This was beginning to become a regular thing. He drank more and more every day. There were lapses of memory and blackouts that sometimes lasted for days. Running his hands through his dark blond hair, he tried to figure out when his life had gone down the toilet. It was an exercise he'd gone through a number of times lately, and one that always brought him full circle to the same conclusions. He had retired from the only life he had known for twenty-six years. It was what Charlotte had wanted, and he had gone along with it. After all, she had spent twenty-three of those twenty-six with him, and he felt he owed her a real home. It would be a place where she could plant roses, if she wanted to, and not have to worry that they would receive orders and be gone before the plants had a chance to bloom. Jake had realized that once he was out, there would be no coming back. His age, the numerous wounds, and the pins and bolts that held his war-torn body together would work against him returning. He had known all of this, yet he had been determined to make it work on the outside. Jake McKenna had given it his best shot and missed.

The adjustment to the civilian way of doing things had been harder than even he had expected. At first, it was just a few drinks at night to help him relax. Before long it began to take more and more, until finally he would finish off an entire bottle before bed. In the end, it had driven away the only thing he had ever really loved. The restraint he was forced to adhere to at work would build resentment within him and be unleashed when he came home and was halfway through a bottle. Fights became a nightly thing around the McKenna household, with him yelling at Charlotte or the kids and throwing furniture around the room or punching holes in the walls. For Charlotte and the kids, Jake's retirement had become a nightmare.

One night, after one of the regular fights, Jake had run out of liquor. He stumbled out to his car. His son, Jason, came out and tried to stop him from driving. Jake still didn't remember what exactly had happened, but he was told that when Jason attempted to take his car keys, he hit his son and knocked him to the ground. The next day he missed work and awoke from his hangover to find Charlotte and the kids were gone.

The letter she left for him brought tears to his

eyes as he read it. No matter how mad she must have been when she left, he knew this had been the hardest thing she had ever had to do. She loved him like no other woman could; however, even the strongest love had to be returned.

They had only talked on the phone twice in the last five months. She was sorry, but until he got some help for his problem, things could never work out between them. She had the kids to think of. Jason had told her to tell his dad that no matter what had happened he still loved him. Jake contacted the Retirement Branch in Indiana and had his checks sent to her and the kids. They lost money on the sale of the house, but he sent her everything from the sale of the furniture and the cars.

Things went steadily downhill after that. He lost his job. He was almost convicted of the murder of the two drug dealers, his only saving grace his Medal of Honor. The Florida prosecutor was afraid it would bring him a ton of bad press if he pushed for a trial: "War hero and Medal of Honor winner on trial for killing of two drug pushers." Where was he going to find twelve people who would convict the man after reading that? All of this left Jake McKenna at the bottom of the barrel. His life was going to hell in a hand basket, and he had reached the point where he didn't really give a damn anymore.

Turning the bottle up to his lips, he took a long pull on the Jack Daniel's. Jake's only friend for the moment burned its way down his throat and once again worked its deadly magic on his mind, convincing him that as long as they had each other, to hell with the rest of the fucking world.

* * *

Sharon snuggled closer to Stryker's warm, naked body. Their long hours of lovemaking had left them both exhausted. Paul and Buck had searched every bar in town and finally returned to the Rustic at ten that night. They had talked to a few people who said they had seen Jake with some long-legged brunette, but they had no idea where the two had been going after they left the bar.

Pete and Doc had arrived on time. Finding no one there to meet them, they had taken a cab into town and went straight to the Rustic, where Sharon filled them in on the situation with Jake. The two were waiting at the bar when Buck and Stryker came back. Doc made three trips to Jake's room but found no one there. Stacks of messages had been left at the front desk. Repeated calls to the desk clerk received the same reply: No, Mr. Mc-Kenna was not in. Sharon finally convinced Paul to give up the search until morning. They all agreed.

Feeling the warmth of her soft body pressed against him, Stryker lightly ran his fingers over her smooth hip and up the curve of her back. The gentle touch brought a low moan from her in her sleep. Her softness began to stir his desire for her once more. Brushing his lips over her hair, he inhaled the sweet smell of her. He needed her again. His hand moved slowly to cup a firm breast.

A sharp knock on the door startled her awake, ruining the mood of the moment for Stryker.

"Goddamnit," he muttered as he pulled his nude body out of the bed. Wrapping a towel around his waist, he went to the door.

Sharon rubbed the sleep from her eyes as she sat up, saying, "That could be Jake."

"If it is, I owe him a shot in the mouth."

Sharon broke out in an uncontrollable laugh. Stryker stopped in the middle of the room. Looking at her, he asked, "You find something funny?"

She couldn't speak as she continued to laugh. Bringing her hand up, she pointed to the towel around his waist. Stryker looked down. He had a massive erection, and the towel protruded out like a circus tent on its side. By the time he looked back at her, she had pulled the sheet over her head, but he could still hear the little-girl giggles coming from under the sheet.

There was another knock on the door. More forceful this time. Self-conscious about his towel, Stryker stood sideways by the door as he opened it slightly. It was Buck. "Damn, Buck. This had better be important."

Buck pushed his way through the door and walked into the room as he said, "It is important, Paul." Glancing over at the bed, he saw Sharon sitting up with the sheet over her head.

"Sorry, Sharon, but this couldn't wait."

"No problem, Bucky," came the reply from under the covers.

Stryker noted the seriousness in Buchanan's eyes as he spoke. "Paul, I just got a call from Randy York. He wants us to meet him and Colonel Richards at the Sheraton Hotel at noon."

Stryker glanced down at his watch. It was ten in the morning. He had not realized it was so late, but then it had been a long exhausting night.

"Colonel Richards—you mean Colonel Erin

Richards, our old Delta Force commander?'' asked Stryker.

"Yeah, the one and only.''

"And you say Randy York is here too?''

"Sure enough. Just got off the phone with him. He—''

Placing his hands on his hips and with a hint of irritation in his voice, Stryker said, "Damn, Buck, you got me outta bed just to tell me that? Hell, they'll be hundreds of guys in town in the next few days. Everybody will have a chance to get together and tell old war stories before the convention's over.''

For the first time since entering the room, Buck noticed the towel. "I see my timing was piss-poor as usual.'' This brought another round of giggles from under the sheet.

"Listen, Paul, Randy's call wasn't for a social get-together. He said it was business and that time was a factor. People's lives are involved.''

Sharon stopped laughing and slowly stuck her head out from under the covers. A frightened look etched its way across her pretty face.

"Why in the hell didn't you say that in the first place?'' boomed Stryker as he pulled the towel off and headed into the shower.

"I was trying to, asshole, but as usual, you cut me off before I could finish. Jeeze! You're a real bitch in the mornings, ain't you?''

"Did Randy say anything about Doc and Pete coming along for this get-together?''

Buck stood in the bathroom doorway. Raising his voice to be heard over the water beating against the shower curtain, he said, "I told him they were here with us. He thought it would be better if just you and I met with them first. If we want in on the deal, we can brief Doc and Pete later.''

"Okay," yelled Stryker. "You got any idea what we might be dealing with, Buck?"

"Not the slightest, Paul."

The shower stopped. Stryker stood drying himself as he said, "Buck, I want you to go back to your room and flip on CNN news. See what the big stories have been in the last twenty-four hours. It might give us an idea of what's going on."

"Sure thing, Paul. Come on over when you're ready to leave."

Stryker nodded as Buck left. Walking to the closet, he removed the unpacked suitcase and began laying out his clothes.

Sharon sat with her arms wrapped around her uplifted knees, silently watching him. "Isn't Erin Richards the colonel you and Buck were with on that hostage-rescue business in Iran?"

"Same one. He's a hell of a commander," said Stryker as he pulled his socks on.

"I thought he retired about the same time you did."

"He did. Matter of fact, he was the one who convinced Randy York to retire at the same time. They put their money together and opened up a high-speed security outfit in L.A."

She couldn't hide the disappointment in her voice as she asked, "Paul, whatever this . . . this thing is, it's going to take you away from me again, isn't it?"

He looked down at her as he buttoned his shirt. The weeks together that he had promised her had only lasted a few hours. He knew she wanted to scream at him to please let this thing go and stay with her, but she wouldn't do that. She knew him too well. He would go, and nothing she could say would stop him.

Sitting on the edge of the bed, he reached out and pulled her to him. Her head rested in the hollow of his strong shoulder. "Oh, Paul, will there ever be a time for us?"

Gently running his fingers through her soft flowing hair, he hugged her tightly to him. He could feel the dampness of her silent tears penetrate his shirt. They had gone through this many times before, but this time it was different. For the first time, he was the one finding it harder to make himself pull away.

"Sharon, I . . . I have to at least go see them. I owe the colonel that much."

"Oh, I know, darling. I just wish that you'd . . . you'd . . . oh, never mind."

The pleading in her words touched him. It was only then that he realized how much he really loved this woman. Yet, he could not remember the last time he had said those words to her. Those words rang commitment. A commitment he was not ready to make right now.

"Sharon, I am going to meet with them, and if we can help the colonel, I'm going to."

Lowering her head so that he would not see her tears, she whispered, "I know, Paul. I wouldn't expect anything less of you."

Standing, he leaned over and kissed her lightly on the forehead, then he went out the door. Hearing the door click shut behind him, Sharon buried her face in the pillow and sobbed quietly. She couldn't help herself. She loved him so much. She had lost him once before because of her foolish pride. Now, she could sense that he was drawing close to her as he had in the beginning, so long ago. The thought of losing him again tore at her heart and brought on a new wave of tears.

Stryker tapped on Buck's door, then entered. Buck was sitting on the bed watching the news.

"Anything look promising, Buck?"

"Not really, Paul, just the standard bullshit. Israel and the Arabs are at it again over the West Bank. Mrs. Aquino has some problems with the guerrillas, but the lady in yellow seems to be handling it okay."

"How about Central America?" asked Stryker.

"Nope. That's a no-go. The five presidents of the big C.A. are meeting in Costa Rica trying to knock out some kind of peace plan. That whole area is in a cease-fire mode right now."

Stryker sat down on the bed and lit a cigarette as he said, "Well, I've never known the colonel or York to cry wolf unless there was a fox in the henhouse. If they say people's lives are involved, then it has to be something they're trying to keep the lid on with a press blackout."

"Sounds like it," said Buck as he grabbed his windbreaker off the back of a chair and turned off the television. "Reckon there ain't no sense in sittin' here guessing. Let's head on over to the Sheraton, get some coffee, and something to eat while we wait for 'em."

Stryker considered taking Sharon along with them, but then changed his mind. He would have to ask her to leave when the colonel arrived. He had already hurt her once this morning; he didn't want to think about having to do it again. He'd stop by the room for a minute just to tell her he loved her. After all, that was how he really felt about her— No, he couldn't do that either. It just wasn't the right time.

"You gonna sit there and wait for 'Sesame Street' to come on so you can learn a few new words or are we going to get somethin' to eat?"

"What? Oh! Let's go get something to eat and some coffee while we wait for them."

As they went out the door, Buck said, "Gee, I wish I would have thought of that."

While Buck went to get the car, Stryker went to Room 317 and knocked on the door. There was no answer. Jake McKenna was still not in.

Randy York put the last suitcase in place and closed the trunk. Moving to the front of the car, he slid in behind the wheel, drove the limousine away from the Learjet and out the V.I.P. exit of the Fayetteville airport.

In the spacious confines behind the driver, retired colonel Erin Richards swung open the well-stocked bar as he said, "I realize it is only ten-thirty in the morning, but you gentlemen have had a long flight. Could I interest you in a drink?"

The distinguished-looking, silver-haired man in his late fifties who sat across from him asked, "Do you have any plain grapefruit juice in there, Colonel?"

"Most assuredly, sir."

Dropping two ice cubes into a glass, Richards popped the top on a small can of the juice and poured half the contents over the ice. Leaning forward, he passed the glass to Johnathan Randolph. Richards caught himself admiring the man's tailor-made charcoal gray suit, and the gold Presidential Rolex that the man wore on his left wrist. The voice was pleasant but tired.

"Thank you, Colonel."

"No problem, sir," said Richards as he turned his attention to the round-faced, mild-looking man who sat to the right of Randolph. His name was Edward Burford; he was the vice president of Randolph Industries. Richards guessed the man to be in his early fifties. Mr. Burford seemed perfectly comfortable in his expensive tailor-cut blue suit.

"Mr. Burford, would you like something, sir?"

"No thank you, Colonel. My stomach has not adjusted from the flight, but thank you for the offer."

Derek Novak, Randolph's chief of security, replied before Richards had a chance to ask. "Nothing for me either, Mr. Richards!"

Novak was a strong-looking man with a big neck and broad shoulders in his early forties. His snug-fitting black suit set perfectly on his six-foot-four frame.

Randolph waited until the colonel had prepared himself a glass of grapefruit juice with a small shot of vodka before he asked, "Colonel, have you made contact with your people yet?"

Richards could feel Novak's eyes on him as he answered, "Yes sir, we have a meeting at noon today with the two men I hope will consent to lead this operation."

"Colonel," said Burford as he shifted slightly in his seat, "I telexed our main office in Bangkok before the flight. The funds you requested will be handled through the American Express Bank. I must admit, they were just as curious as I was about your request that the sum you asked for be made in gold leaf ounces, rather than cash.''

"I assure you, sir, there was a specific reason for that request. We're going to have to spread a lot of money around when we get to Thailand. Too many bills showing up at once could draw unwanted attention. People tend to horde gold more than cash. The Thais prefer gold to paper money any day.'' The hard stare he was receiving from Novak was becoming annoying. Looking over at the big man, Richards asked, "Is there a problem, Mr. Novak?''

The security chief sat ramrod straight, his big hands resting on his knees.

"I suppose I still have some reservations about the people you have contacted to handle this affair.'' Leaning forward and interlocking his fingers, Novak continued, "I'll be quite honest with you, Mr. Richards. I strongly advised Mr. Randolph to withhold that telex to Bangkok until I had an opportunity to interview your people personally and make a judgment as to their qualifications.''

Randolph removed his sunglasses as he said, "Mr. Novak, we've already gone over that and I—''

Erin Richards raised his hand. "No. That's quite all right, Mr. Randolph.''

Richards noticed the marked emphasis Novak placed on addressing him as Mr. Richards—rather than Colonel, as Randolph and Burford had done. Richards had already checked out the security boss. Novak had spent fifteen years in the Marine Corps and had been selected for the lieutenant colonel's list when he resigned his commission to take the security job with Randolph Industries. The money he now made was enough to turn a general green with envy. Yet no one called him "Colonel" Novak. There seemed to be an unspoken sense of resentment on Novak's part because of that. Leaning forward to assure eye-to-eye contact with the security chief, Richards said, "Mr. Novak, I can personally assure you that the men I have in mind for this operation are the best in the business."

A slight smirk formed at the corner of Novak's lips as he replied, "You obviously place considerable faith in your judgment of men and their abilities, Mr. Richards. Unfortunately, it is Mr. Randolph who must depend on that judgment and his daughter who will pay the price if you are wrong."

Randy York averted his eyes from the road for a moment, glancing up into the rearview mirror for the colonel's reaction to Novak's statement. It wasn't long in coming.

"I would remind you, sir, that it was a lack of ability and judgment on the part of your security people that brought about this situation."

Grinning, Randy York turned his attention back to the road, whispering quietly to himself, "That's telling the prick, Colonel."

Novak's fingers instantly balled into two massive fists as they rested on his knees. Richards could see the veins in the man's neck bulge. He could feel the hatred in Novak's eyes. There had been no sarcasm in Richards's remark. It was made in a simple, matter-of-fact tone.

Burford watched nervously as the two ex-military men stared hard at one another across the short span between the seats. The tension could be felt in the confines of the car. Edward Burford had no desire to be caught in the middle of a confrontation between these two men who were accustomed to violence. My God! They'd destroy him in place.

It was the calm but weary voice of Johnathan Randolph that defused the situation. "Gentlemen, if you don't mind, I would prefer that you put aside any personal differences you may have until we have taken care of the matter at hand—which I believe is the rescue and safe return of my daughter."

Without taking his eyes off Richards, Novak slowly relaxed his clenched fingers and sat back in his seat. The colonel also sat back, silently cursing himself for having allowed the confrontation to occur.

Johnathan Randolph replaced his sunglasses and stared out at the North Carolina countryside as the group rode in silence.

A huge sign came up on the left: TWIN LAKES COUNTRY CLUB, HOME OF RAY BOYD, SIX-TIME PGA CHAMPION. York swung the long limo into the circle drive that led up and around the oval containing thousands of multicolored flowers. Passing the clubhouse, he drove another quarter of a mile until they came to a set of wrought-iron gates. Two men in dark windbreakers approached the car as it came to a stop. York lowered the window as the larger of the two men came up to him. York smiled as he asked, "Everything okay, Bobby Joe?"

The husky young man with the corn silk hair returned the smile, and in a heavy southern accent answered, " 'Bout as quiet as a whore in church, Major."

From the back seat, Richards asked, "Any problem with curious club members, Bobby?"

The Georgia boy took a couple of steps back to

the rear of the car and assumed a position of attention, more from reflex than necessity.

"No sir, we had a few autograph seekers but we told 'em the Boyds were out of the country and we were private security hired to watch the house."

"Good job, Bobby. We'll be at the house. Any problems, call me."

"Yes sir, Colonel," said Bobby Joe as he waved to the guard inside to open the gates.

As York eased the car past the gate, Novak turned and looked out the back window. The man who had opened the gates had a Mac-10 machine gun resting snugly on the back of his belt. No doubt, Bobby Joe and the other man outside the gates were equally armed.

To call the Boyd residence a house would be a gross understatement. It was more like a mansion. Standing two stories high, it had four large white pillars in the front. It was typical of the old southern mansions of a bygone era. There were ten bedrooms, each with its own full bath. There was a huge den with a large open fireplace and elaborate furnishings, a study, a library, and an extravagant living room two times larger than a basketball court. In the back was the pool, a hot tub, and two greenhouses.

The Boyds and the Randolphs had been friends for years. When Randolph had contacted Richards for help, the colonel related that one of the first problems they were going to encounter would be finding a location where they could quietly and tactfully organize and plan an operation without drawing a lot of attention and unwanted questions. Randolph had immediately called the Boyds, who were on a trip in England. Within the hour, Randolph had full use of the estate, no questions asked. The staff were given a one-week vacation with two weeks' pay, courtesy of Randolph Industries.

York waved to three of the guards who were patrolling the grounds to help carry the luggage inside. Richards directed the visitors to their rooms. Lunch would be prepared whenever they were ready to eat. If they needed anything, they could ask any of the guards in the house.

Randolph thanked the colonel as he and Novak made their way up the spiral staircase to the second floor. Edward Burford paused a moment as he started up the steps and stared at the 9-mm Beretta strapped on the belt of the man carrying his bags. His eyes lingered on the flat black finish of the weapon which he knew served only one purpose. He was not a man prone to violence. He had never been in the military, nor had he ever had the desire to be. Guns scared him, and the very thought of using one on another human being sent shivers down his spine. As they reached the top of the stairs, Burford noticed the colonel and York going into the study. Within the next few days, those two men would plan an operation for other men like them. By the time this was over, people were going to be killed. From what Burford had learned of Colonel Richards and his staff, it was a profession at which they were very efficient.

The waitress finished pouring the coffee and asked the new arrivals if they would like to order. Richards and York both declined. Stryker took advantage of the moment to study his former commander.

Erin Richards was fifty-four years old. His black

hair was beginning to show telltale signs of graying along the sides. His yellow polo shirt fit well over his athletic chest. The short sleeves were stretched to the limit around his strong muscular arms. The ol' man had kept himself in good shape. The same was true of Randy York. He was the same age as Stryker. His dark brown hair and soft brown eyes accented his ruggedly handsome face. It was a face that would remind people of the cowboy from the Marlboro cigarette commercials.

Stryker waited until the waitress had left before he began.

"Colonel, what can we do for you?"

Richards glanced around the room to assure that no one was close enough to overhear. Stryker had purposely picked a table away from the main flow of the dining room. They were totally alone.

"Paul, I've got one hell of a problem on my hands and damn little time to solve it."

"Well, sir, you know if there's anything Buck and I can do to help you out, you got it."

"Thanks, Paul. I was hoping you'd say that. Are either of you familiar with an outfit called Randolph Industries?"

Buck answered, "Megabucks outfit. Big in the oil business overseas. Offshore drilling, tankers, that kind of stuff."

"Lately they've invested heavily in the gold and copper markets as well as diamond interests in South Africa," added Stryker.

Richards seemed pleased with their answers, as Buck asked, "What about them, Colonel?"

"Two days ago, the Na Pho refugee camp in Thailand was attacked and four American women were kidnapped; three were Catholic nuns and the fourth was Denise Randolph, the daughter of the founder and owner of Randolph Industries.''

"Holy shit," said Buck.

"Somebody must be keeping the lid on pretty tight, Colonel. We haven't seen or heard a thing about this on the news," said Stryker as he took a sip of his coffee.

Randy York leaned back in his chair as he said, "Johnathan Randolph has been in touch with our embassy people and the Thai government. They're trying to keep it nailed down, but it's only a matter of time before someone leaks the news. You guys know how that shit goes. Once that happens, we're really going to have a tough time getting those people back. You see, Paul, whoever snatched those women has no idea that they have the daughter of one of the richest men in the country.''

"I take it we have no confirmation of who, or how many people were involved in this attack, right?'' asked Stryker.

"That's correct, Paul," said Richards. "Rick Alley's working on that for me right now. I'm expecting a call from him this afternoon.''

Stryker seemed surprised to hear the name.

"Rick Alley! I thought he left the CIA a couple of years ago?''

"He did. He married a Thai girl and bought himself a bar in Bangkok. He still has a lot of contacts with the Agency boys and the Thai secret police," said Richards.

Stryker sat silent for a moment as if deep in thought before he said, "Colonel, you already have a pretty good idea who took those people and where they are right now, don't you?''

"I've got a few ideas, Paul. Why don't you tell me who you think pulled this off?"

Stryker spoke without looking up from his coffee cup, "Laotians, either Pathet Lao or bandits, and they've moved those women back across the border into Laos."

"My feeling exactly," said the colonel. "Rick's call this afternoon should confirm that."

"What do the State Department boys have to say about all this?" asked Buck.

Richards shook his head. "I'm afraid what we've got here is a damn catch-22 situation. The State Department can't do anything but issue the same bullshit protest and demands for the release of our people. The Thais can't go sweeping into Laos to attempt a rescue without having to take on the twenty-five or thirty thousand North Vietnamese troops that are stationed there. Hanoi would love nothing better than a reason to scream invasion and start another Southeast Asian war."

Stryker rubbed his chin a moment, then looked across at Richards as he said, "Colonel, this Johnathan Randolph is a multimillionaire. I'm sure he has a lot of friends on Capitol Hill. Can't they push a few buttons and get somebody on this?"

"He's already tried that, Paul," said York. "The few senators he could trust not to leak the news were sorry as hell about his situation, but they couldn't do anything for him. They referred him back to the State Department. Keep in mind, boys, this is an election year."

"What about the Delta Force?" asked Buck. "This isn't much different than a hostage situation. It should be right up their alley."

"No, Buck, not quite. A plane hijacking in the

Middle East, or a hostage deal in Europe, that's one thing, but the minute you mention putting U.S. ground troops of any kind back in Southeast Asia, people start screaming about another Vietnam War. The Senate and the Congress would crucify the President," said Richards.

"Well then, it would seem our Mr. Randolph is between the ol' rock and a hard place, don't it," said Buck.

"You've got it," said Richards, nodding his head. "We've tried the legal and official channels, but so far every door we've knocked on has been shut in our face. Everybody's sorry as hell, but they can't do anything about it. Mr. Randolph doesn't want to hear that. He just wants his little girl back, safe and sound, and he doesn't care what it costs."

"How'd you get involved in this, Colonel?" asked Stryker.

"One of the senators Randolph contacted suggested that he get in touch with my office. He hinted, unofficially of course, that this was the type of problem that we specialized in. Randy and I went to see him that morning. Once we heard the story, I called Rick in Bangkok and got the ball rolling. Rick mentioned that you boys had been canceled out on your African contracts and were planning to be in Fayetteville for the convention. You've both spent a lot of time in that part of the world. We just figured you might want a shot at this one. Like I said, Mr. Randolph doesn't care what it costs. This would pay the bills for a mighty long time. So what d'you think? Are you in?"

A silence fell over the table as Stryker and Buchanan exchanged glances across the table. It wasn't the kind of break they had planned on; but then, Denise Randolph hadn't planned on being carried off by a bunch of gun-toting guerrillas, either.

"Well, what do think, partner? You feel up to another trip to the exotic, mystical lands of Southeast Asia?" asked Stryker.

An ornery smile came over Buck's face as he leaned back and said, "What the hell! I could make enough off this run to retire to that bar stool out there in the pines. Why not? Let's do it."

Stryker turned to Richards. "Looks like you got yourself a deal, Colonel. I'd like to be with you when you get that call from Rick this afternoon. I'll need to know what we're up against so I'll know how many people I'm going to need. Doc Shannon and Pete Merrill are already here. I'm pretty sure they'll want in on this."

"Of course, Paul. I brought some of my security people along. They're young, but they're good. You might want to check a few of them out. But of course, personnel selection is up to you. It's your show," said Richards.

"Thank you, sir. If they work for you, I'm sure they're good people."

Buck leaned forward on the table as he looked over at Stryker and said, "You know, Paul, there's one guy in town right now who could provide a big edge for us on this thing."

The colonel and York stared at Buck with questioning eyes.

"You're right, Buck," answered Stryker. "Jake McKenna—Jesus, the guy spent five years in Laos working with the Ravens and the White Star proj-

ects. He knows that country like the back of his
hand.''

"You got it. Jake was practically a legend among
the Meo tribesmen. I'll bet he's still got a lot of
friends livin' up in those mountains. It wouldn't
take him long to put a respectable-size army together to give us a hand.''

Stryker saw the look of concern on the colonel's
face. "Is something wrong, sir?'' he asked.

Richards seemed uncomfortable with the question as he answered. "You may want to reconsider
bringing Jake in on this, Paul. From what I've been
hearing, Jake's not the same man we used to
know.''

A deep frown worked its way across Stryker's
face.

"With all due respect, sir, Jake McKenna is one
of the best damn soldiers I ever had the privilege
to work with. I don't have to remind you that he
got that CMH for dragging me and three other guys
out of a burning helicopter; then he held off a whole
platoon of NVA by himself. Hell, we were all so
fucked up we couldn't do a thing to help him. By
the time help got there, Jake was shot to hell, but
he never gave it up. I know what you're saying,
Colonel, I've heard he's been having a tough time
of it right now, but damn, sir. I guess what I'm
trying to say is, Jake was there when I needed him.
Now, maybe I can return the favor.''

There was a slight hint of doubt in Richards's
voice as he said, "I hope you're right, Paul. I hear
the only thing he's been battling lately is the bottle.
I don't have to remind you of what could happen
if he talked to the wrong people. This entire op-

eration could be shut down before it ever gets off the ground.''

"I realize that, sir.''

"Okay, then, Paul, you're the main man. You do whatever you feel is right.''

Richards slid his chair back and stood up. The others stood as well. Reaching his hand across the table, the colonel took Stryker's in his own.

"Paul, we're staying at the Boyd estate out at Twin Lakes Country Club. Are you familiar with the place?''

"Yes, sir. As a matter of fact, you and I played a round of golf out there a few years back.''

"By golly, that's right. That seems like another century now. Well, you come about five. I'm expecting Rick's call around six. You'll have a chance to meet Mr. Randolph and a couple of his associates.''

"Sounds good, sir. See you at five.''

York shook hands with both men; then he followed the colonel out the door. Stryker tossed a twenty-dollar bill on the table.

"Come on, Buck. We've got a lot to do before five.''

"Where are we off to, Paul?'' asked Buck as they walked across the lobby.

"First we're going to round up Doc and Pete; then we're going to turn this town upside down and see if we can shake Jake McKenna out of the cracks.''

As they crossed the parking lot, Buck remarked, "You know, the ol' man made it sound like maybe Jake's kind of lost it. You know what I mean?''

"Yeah, I know. That's why we have to find him.

The only thing that's going to keep him from killing himself is a chance to get killed with us!''

''Say what?'' exclaimed Buck. ''Ya wanta run that one by me one more time?''

Stryker didn't bother to answer as he slid in behind the wheel and started the car. Buck Buchanan was still thinking about Stryker's remark as they pulled out of the parking lot.

Chapter 5

The early morning fog had begun to burn off with the rising sun. The base camp slowly stirred to life as the troops of Colonel Bao crawled from beneath their ponchos and made their way to the edge of the jungle to relieve themselves. Others brought smoldering coals to life in preparation for the morning meal.

In the poncho and palm-leaf lean-to that sat near the center of the camp, Denise Randolph slowly opened her eyes. The cold dampness of the ground caused an aching in her legs. Her hands were still tied tightly behind her back. A burning sensation shot through her shoulder blades as she struggled to sit up. Finding the effort too painful, she lowered her head back to the damp ground. The stinging sensation she felt along the side of her face was brought on by the numerous scratches that ran along her cheeks and forehead. The small cuts and nicks had been made by the cutting edges of the leaves and vines that struck her face as she had been pushed, dragged and pulled through the jungle over the last twenty-four hours.

Once again she closed her eyes and dared hope against hope that this was all just a terrible nightmare that would finally end when she opened them again.

A hand grabbed the front of her shirt and jerked her upright. The pain that shot through her arms and the middle of her back shattered any illusions that this was only a bad dream.

As the blinding pain slowly cleared, she found herself staring into the face of Colonel Bao. His coal-black hair covered his ears. His eyes were as black as his hair. She could feel the cold, calculating stare move over her face and down her body. A long ugly scar ran down his left cheek, ending at his lower lip. Tobacco-stained teeth showed through his self-satisfied grin as he reached out and undid the top button of her shirt. Fighting to control her emotions, she tried to hide the fear that welled up within her, but her eyes were betraying her.

Denise felt a slight breeze touch her breast as another button gave way to his rough and dirty fingers. Bao's smile broadened as he undid a third. His black eyes were taking in the softness of her smooth breasts that pushed outward against the restraint of her white lace bra. Running his finger lightly along the edge of the lace, he looked up at her. His voice was hard. "What is your name, woman?"

His finger stopped in the valley of her breasts, sending a chill through her. She tried to speak but couldn't. Those cold dead eyes and the fear pounding through her choked off any words. Pulling on the front of her bra, he laughed as he watched the firm breasts bounce gracefully up and down.

"So you have no name. Then I shall have to give you one—let's see now, what shall we call you?"

Removing his finger from her bra, he undid another button. Only one remained. Bao brought his hand up, spreading his fingers wide. Reaching into her shirt, he covered her left breast with the big hand. Denise felt a sudden cramping in the pit of her stomach. She was going to be sick. The fingers tightened as he leaned forward, nibbled at her ear, and whispered, "Maybe I should call you . . . Cunt! Yes, my beautiful, American Cunt! Do you like that?"

The hand tightened even more, sending a ripple of pain through her entire body.

"Or perhaps you prefer Bitch!" he said as his tongue snaked out at her ear.

Pulling her head away from him, she cried out, "No! No! Please leave me alone. . . . Please!"

"Oh, no, my beauty," he said as he twisted his hand even tighter and more cruelly this time. "I have already waited too long. I may do many things to you today, but leaving you alone is not one of them."

Releasing her breast, his hand shot out, slapping her along the side of the face. The blow knocked Denise on her side. Bao tore the last remaining button from her shirt and opened it wide. Pulling a knife from his boot, he slid it up between her breasts and cut away the bra. Her small, firm breasts were now exposed to him. She screamed and fought to get away from him, but it was a useless effort.

His rough hands squeezed and pulled at her soft chest. Dropping his head onto her breast, he bit at her nipples as she jerked from the sharp pain. The soldiers in the camp began to gather around their commander and cheer him on as their lust-filled eyes lingered on her naked chest.

Bao's desire for the woman was out of control. Slapping her again, he straddled her legs. With both hands, he tore open the front of her pants, exposing a pair of white lace panties. This sight brought another cheer from the bandits around her. Bao's breathing became heavy. For a woman of such limited size, she was showing remarkable strength. A savage slap to her left cheek stalled her resistance. Hooking his fingers into the waistband of the pants, he violently pulled them down to her knees. Denise screamed, "Oh my God. No! Please, no!"

Rising to his knees, Bao grinned as he undid his belt and began opening the front of his pants. His hands were shaking in anticipation. He could barely control himself.

The sudden rattle of automatic weapons fire sent Bao diving off the girl and into a corner of the lean-to. The cheering observers dropped flat to the ground while others scrambled for their weapons and cover.

Peering out from the corner of the makeshift shelter, Bao saw three men standing in the center of his camp. The tall Russian who had fired the AK-47 into the air was now lowering the weapon back down to his side. Glancing over at the almost naked body of the American girl, Bao cussed under his breath as he pulled himself from the shelter. Buttoning his pants as he made his way toward the three visitors, he uttered to himself, "She is prime. It will be there later."

The Russian was Colonel Ivan Kloskov, senior advisor to the two North Vietnamese officers who stood on either side of him with their hands on their hips. Bao could see the look of contempt on the faces of the Communist leaders as he approached the group. The feeling was mutual. Bao hated the Russians and could barely tolerate the North Vietnamese. It was a limited tolerance that was necessary, only because they kept him supplied with weapons and ammunition. In return, his ragtag, but efficient, army conducted harassment actions against the Thais and patrolled the isolated areas along the northern Laotian border.

Giving a halfhearted salute, Bao smiled as he asked, "Comrades! To what do I owe this great honor?"

Colonel Nuhgen Van Diem was the district leader for the Khammouane Province. It was the province that contained Bao's main guerrilla operations base. He did not acknowledge the attempted salute, nor did the other two officers. Diem's voice teetered on the verge of yelling. "Is that one of the women from Na Pho?"

A look of innocence came over Bao's face; there was a certain cockiness in his voice as he replied, "Na Pho, Comrade? What would I know of Na Pho?"

Major Qhan Thieu, commander of the NVA units under Diem's supervision, moved his hand to the holster that hung at his side as he snarled, "You insolent son of a dog!"

The Russian grabbed Thieu's hand before he could pull the weapon. "Major! There is no need for that."

Thieu saw Kloskov nod slightly when he spoke. Looking slowly around him, Thieu saw the guns of Bao's army leveled at them. Kloskov released the man's hand, then smiled at Bao. "Captain Bao. I—"

Bao raised his hand as he interrupted. "It is not Captain Bao—it is Colonel! Comrade. I was a captain when I served my NVA brothers in the service of the Pathet Lao. Following our great victory, my NVA leaders neglected to recognize my superior leadership." Pausing to focus his catty smile on Colonel Diem, he continued. "A misfortunate loss of paperwork, I'm sure. Therefore, I found it necessary to promote myself. So, my Russian friend, you will please address me as Colonel Bao. You may now continue, Colonel Kloskov."

Kloskov fought back the urge to reach out and tear the man's head from his shoulders. To him, Bao was no more a colonel than he was a professional soldier. The bastard was nothing more than a renegade bandit who fed on the misery and suffering of the helpless. He had managed to gather the scum of Laos around him to form the nucleus of his bandit army. Remarkably, the army numbered close to 700 men. A formidable force when armed with modern weapons. Bao's only loyalty was to himself. When he split from the Patho Lao army, he began attacking not only the Thais but the government troops of the new Communist party in Laos. Two NVA convoys had been ambushed by unknown forces in the last five months. Colonel Diem was convinced that Bao was behind the attacks, but he could not prove that charge. It had been the Russians who proposed a truce between Bao and the new government. Rather than fighting each other, they had engineered the constructive use of Bao's forces. They used them against the Thais and as a source of security along the mountain range areas of the Laotian border. It was against their better judgment, but to please their

Russian comrades the NVA had agreed to the truce and provided Bao with tons of weapons and ammunition. Once he was fully armed, both the Russians and the NVA found they had no control over the man's actions. The senseless attack against the refugee camp was a perfect example.

Regaining his composure, Colonel Kloskov began again. ''Colonel Bao, less than thirty-six hours ago the Na Pho refugee camp was attacked and five Americans were killed, one of them a priest. Four American women were also kidnapped. The Thai losses in the attack were considerable. For some reason that we cannot yet explain, the American and Thai governments have not released any information about this event to the press. However, I can assure you that Moscow, as well as Hanoi and the government of Laos, has already received very disturbing messages from the American State Department about this affair. My superiors, as well as Colonel Diem's, have ordered that we investigate this incident and report our findings immediately.''

Bao slowly stroked his chin as he listened to Kloskov. He was trying to figure a way to justify his actions at Na Pho and still come out of this thing with something of value. Stalling for time, Bao continued the cat-and-mouse game.

''I can see your point, Colonel. The killing of Americans is one thing, but the killing of a priest— a holy man of God—that is truly a terrible thing. The abduction of helpless women is even worse. Such a thing would surely bring forth a cry of outrage from the international community, wouldn't you say so, Colonel Diem?''

Colonel Diem's answer was filled with sarcasm. "Most assuredly . . . Comrade!"

Bao looked down at the ground as he slowly moved the toe of his boot along the leaves. He could never justify the attack. He knew that. It had simply been an act committed out of sheer boredom. The capture of the four women had been an unexpected bonus. He had planned to keep them for his amusement for a few weeks, then sell them back to the rich Catholic order that had sent them to Na Pho. But now, maybe he could save himself the trouble of dealing with the Church. He would sell them to the Russians. Looking up at Kloskov, he said, "What if I could help you with this problem? I mean, suppose I could locate the people who have done this thing? And if . . . and I say only if . . . I can convince them to turn these Americans over to me, what would my men and I gain from this show of loyalty to fellow brothers and comrades?"

Colonel Diem's face turned a crimson red as he fought to control the rage that was welling up within him. The son of a bitch was blackmailing them. Colonel Kloskov stared beyond Bao and at the nude body of the woman who lay sobbing in the corner of the shelter, a piece of her shredded blouse clutched in a vain effort to hide her nakedness. For all the rank and title he held in this country, he now stood in front of this scum, Bao, a man he considered lower than any animal on this earth, and was helpless to do anything.

Major Thieu pointed to the girl as he screamed at the bandit, "That woman is one of those that you kidnapped! Where are the other three, you bastard? The Republic of Vietnam and the people of Laos demand that you release these women to us.''

Bao seemed amused that he had managed to incite the young Vietnamese officer. He smiled as he replied, ''I would have you know, Major, my parents were married, and as far as that woman is concerned, I believe you are mistaken!''

''We shall see!'' said Thieu as he stomped past Bao and walked toward the lean-to. Bao's hand quickly went up into the air. The sound of metal against metal echoed in the jungle as bolts went forward and safety switches clicked to the firing position. Four guerrillas stepped between Thieu and the sobbing girl. Their rifles were pointed at the major's midsection.

Looking back over his shoulder, Bao maintained his cocky, self-assured tone as he spoke. ''As I said, Major, you are mistaken!''

Knowing it would be an act of futility to draw the pistol, Kloskov edged his hand slowly for his holster and braced himself for whatever was going to happen next. He knew Bao was a madman and would think nothing of killing all three of them right here and now.

A silence fell over the camp. No one moved; even the birds in the trees stopped their calling as if they, too, sensed the tension that was building in the small clearing below. Colonel Diem's hand rested on the grip of his Chicom pistol as he silently prayed that Buddha would allow him one shot at Bao before he died.

Colonel Kloskov saw there was nothing to lose and everything to gain by offering Bao a deal. The man, after all, was a bandit. The Russian hoped Bao's greed was stronger than his thirst for blood.

"Colonel Bao, sir! If you could find these missing Americans for us, I can guarantee you that my superiors would consider it a great service worthy of a reward—say in gold, perhaps."

Bao continued to stare at Major Thieu, who now stood motionless, his hand gripping the butt of his pistol. If Bao dropped his arm, the three men would be cut to pieces by a hail of bullets from all sides. Kloskov's mention of gold widened the smile on the bandit's face. The Russian had found Bao's weakness—the bright yellow glow of gold.

Seconds passed as Bao considered the idea of killing only Thieu and Diem. No . . . that would serve no worthwhile purpose. Not that he really cared anyway. However, he knew the Russians would take a dim view of that action and would surely withdraw their offer. That, he did care about.

Instructing Thieu to rejoin the group, he waved his gunmen off as he spoke to Kloskov. "Your offer is a most honorable gesture, Comrade. If you could convince our North Vietnamese allies to furnish an additional shipment of weapons and ammunition, I'm certain we could find all of the American women."

Colonel Diem, the fire now gone from his voice, replied, "I . . . I am sure that can be arranged, Colonel Bao."

Diem's recognition of his rank elicited a cruel grin from Bao. Spitting at Diem's feet, he said, "That will be fine, Colonel. It is a good thing when men of equal stature can work out their differences."

Kloskov asked, "Colonel Bao, could you give me some idea of when the women may be found?"

"The search will begin immediately, Comrade.

I am sure I can locate them and be prepared to turn them over to you within seven days from today.''

"Very well then," said Diem. "We will meet you here in seven days."

"No, Diem, not here. We will meet in the valley of Xieng Khouang, upon the Plain of Jars," said Bao.

"That is ridiculous," said Major Thieu. "It will take me at least three days to gather the weapons and ammunition and to put a convoy together. Then another three days to reach that valley. Why can we not just make the exchange here?"

The smile fell from Bao's face as he looked directly at Kloskov and said, "I prefer a location from which I can be assured that *all* I receive is a shipment of weapons and gold. I am certain our Russian friend understands. Now, Comrades, if you will excuse me. I believe we all have work to do. My men will escort you out of here. We would not want any unfortunate accidents to befall our guest, now would we?"

Kloskov noticed Bao glancing back at the nude girl.

"Colonel Bao, there will be one stipulation before you can receive your gold."

"And what would that be, Comrade?"

"None of the women must be harmed in any way. I am sure you understand what I mean."

Bao nodded reluctantly as he answered, "Comrade Kloskov, are you telling me that the great power of the Russian bear to which we poor Asians owe so much has developed a conscience?" Laughing at his own joke, Bao continued, "Have no fear, your American sluts shall be returned unsoiled, as they say. Now go! You begin to bore me.''

Kloskov clenched his teeth, causing the muscles in his strong, square-set jaw to twitch. His dark brown eyes were alive with the fire of pure hatred for this man. He started to say something then let it go. Further talking would be pointless. But there would be another time and another place. A place more of Kloskov's choosing, and a time when Bao would not have his army to back him up. That was all Kloskov wanted. He was going to kill Bao with his bare hands. The thought of the pleasure that would bring brought a smile to his face as he turned to leave with Diem and Thieu.

Bao returned to the shelter and sat down next to the girl. Running his hand down her bare back, he felt her tremble under his touch. ''Do not fear, my little bitch. As much as I desire your young body, my desire for gold is far stronger. If that means I must forsake the pleasures you have to offer, then so be it.''

His words stilled the trembling within her. Now there was only the silent sobbing which she could not control. Bao continued to talk. ''They think me to be a fool. Yet, I have slowly amassed a fortune through their ignorance. One day I will leave this godforsaken place and live the life I so richly deserve. So, stop your silly crying. The Russian colonel has saved that great treasure you believe you possess between your legs.'' Laughing to himself, Bao stood, tossed a poncho over her and walked away.

Denise Randolph remained huddled in the corner. Bao's words kept resounding through her mind, but made no sense—"The Russian has saved you!"

It was exactly five in the afternoon when Stryker and Buchanan arrived at the Boyd residence. Stryker was in a bad mood. They had not found Jake McKenna. Shannon and Merrill were still searching for him.

The two combat vets spotted the concealed weapons as soon as they approached the gate. The colonel wasn't fooling around; this was a hard site. Stryker was impressed by the tall blond kid at the gate with his no-nonsense attitude and superior methods as he checked out the car and its passengers. He had all the earmarks of a Randy York training session.

Parking in front of the mansion, they went up the front steps. Buck paused a moment to survey the size of the home. "Now, I want ya to look at this place, man. I been to three rodeos, two circuses and a county fair; but brother, I ain't never seen anything like this. Hard to believe a guy could get all this by just hittin' a little ol' white ball around with a damn stick."

"You see, Buck, the trick is to hit it farther and a lot less often than the competition."

Randy York met them at the door.

"Paul . . . Buck, good to see you again. You're right on time. Where's Doc and Pete?"

"They're still trying to locate Jake," said Buck.

"Figured as much. Come on in. The colonel's in the study with Mr. Randolph and his people. There's not much we can do until we get that call from Rick."

As they made their way down the corridor, Stryker asked, "Randy, you and the ol' man handle many jobs like this?"

"Nothing quite this big before, Paul. Mostly basic security, bodyguards, courier and corporate-type jobs. After talking with Randolph, the colonel just couldn't turn this one down. The poor guy didn't have anybody left to turn to. I won't bullshit you, Paul, it's going to be a bloody one."

Stryker and Buchanan looked at each other knowingly as Paul replied, "Never seen one that wasn't, Randy."

Stopping at the door of the study, York said, "Paul, Mr. Randolph is not too familiar with the military aspects of this thing, so if he seems a little confused about something, he may ask a lot of questions."

"If I were in the guy's shoes, I think I would too."

"One more thing, you guys. Randolph's chief of security is a guy named Derek Novak. He's an ex-Marine major. Four of his boys were assigned to protect the boss's daughter. They were all four killed at Na Pho. Novak's a little on the abrasive side, but the guy knows his business or he wouldn't be working for Randolph. He's not too hot on the colonel or our ability to handle this situation."

Buchanan laughed as he said, "Hell, Randy, you're talking to 'Mr. Personality' here. I can get along with anybody. 'Course, I can't say the same for my partner here. I've overheard him saying some really sick things about Marines and their mothers."

Stryker shook his head. "You know, Buck, you're really beginning to be a dick in your old age."

York opened the door to the study and as they went inside he whispered, "Good to see you boys haven't mellowed with the years."

Burford stood by the bar with a drink in his hand. Randolph, Novak, and the colonel were standing in front of a large map of Thailand and Laos that hung on the wall. A small mountain of files and papers covered the top of the solid oak desk next to them. In another part of the room, two of Richards's men were working on a set of charts. The study had been converted into an operations center. The activity in the room came to a halt as everyone turned to look at the new arrivals. Richards smiled as he called across the room, "Paul! Buck! Glad you're here. Come on over here and let me introduce everyone."

"Later guys," said York as he slapped them on the back and went to help with the charts.

Stryker studied the group as he and Buck walked across the room. The three men now standing around Richards were dressed casually, but it was the expensive type of casual that few people could afford: two-hundred-dollar slacks, three-hundred-dollar sweaters and Italian shoes that cost more than the whole outfit put together.

Richards stepped forward and shook hands with both men, then began the introductions. "Paul, this is Johnathan Randolph. Sir, these are two of the finest Special Forces team sergeants it has ever been my pleasure to command. This is Paul Stryker and Buck Buchanan."

Randolph's grip was firm as he said, "Gentlemen, it's a pleasure. I want you both to know I appreciate what you're doing."

"Thank you, sir. We'll do everything possible to get your daughter home, safe and sound."

Richards turned to the short man to Randolph's right. "And this is Mr. Burford, vice president of Randolph Industries."

"It's very nice to meet you, gentlemen," said Burford nervously as he lightly exchanged handshakes, quickly pulling his hand back as if he were afraid the two big men were going to tear it off at the wrist.

The colonel didn't have to introduce the man on the left. Stryker had felt Novak's eyes on them the minute they had entered the room.

"Boys, this is Derek Novak, chief of security for Randolph Industries."

Novak purposely reached past Stryker's outstretched hand and shook hands with Buck first. Stepping back slightly, he then clasped his big hand around Stryker's as he said, "I understand you are quite the guerrilla warfare expert, Mr. Stryker." Novak steadily increased the pressure of his grip as he spoke.

Stryker grinned and began applying a little pressure of his own as he answered. "You might say I've learned a few tricks over the years."

A slight burning sensation began in the palm of Novak's hand as Stryker continued to squeeze harder. Novak tried to pull his hand back, but Stryker held on. With a Cheshire cat grin on his face, he said, "Understand you were a Marine at one time, Mr. Novak. That must be where you got that grip. I hear they masturbate a lot in that outfit."

Stryker gave the hand a final squeeze, then released it. Burford had almost spit his drink on Randolph when Stryker made the last remark. Novak started to say something in return, but a look from Randolph made him reconsider. Instead, he flexed his blood-drained fingers to force feeling back into his hand.

Buck moved to the wall and tapped his finger at a place on the map. "Good ol' Nakhon Phanom. Man, we launched a hell of a lot of missions outta that place, didn't we, Colonel?"

"More than our share, Buck. You boys like a drink?"

"That sounds like a winner to me," said Buck. "How 'bout you, Paul?"

"Yeah, Buck, Jack on the rocks," replied Stryker as he stood looking at the map. The area of Na Pho was blocked in red.

"You know, it's really quite amazing, Mr. Stryker," said Randolph as he moved to Stryker's side.

"What's that, sir?"

"That a man as well educated and intelligent as I am supposed to be has so little knowledge of a country such as Laos."

"You're not alone in that area, sir. There are a lot of people that don't. Laos just never seemed to catch on like Vietnam. Even when Nixon was bombing the hell out of the place, nobody really got concerned about it." Stryker paused, then asked, "Sir, if you don't mind my asking, just what the hell was the daughter of a multimillionaire doing in a place like Na Pho?"

Randolph sighed wearily as he answered. "She was searching for something, Mr. Stryker. Something she felt was missing from her life. I suppose I, like so many other ambitious men who pursue the almighty dollar, became so caught up in that pursuit that I neglected to see what was happening to my daughter. Dealing with millions of dollars a day, buying, selling, trading and always trying to outwit the other guy, always trying to stay on top, you lose sight of the things that mean the most to you. They slip away, and you don't realize what you've lost until it's too late.''

Buck brought the drinks over.

''Thanks, Buck. Mr. Randolph was just explaining how his daughter happened to be in Na Pho.''

''I was wondering about that myself.''

''Please go on, Mr. Randolph,'' said Stryker.

''As I was saying, I was so busy making money over the years that I never really gave it much thought until this happened. The night Denise was born, I was in a meeting that could have marked the collapse of Randolph Industries before it even began. When they told me my wife was in the hospital, I had to make a choice. I elected to stay at the bargaining table and try to save my meager business. Believe me, gentlemen, in those early years it was a meager business. It was a decision I have always regretted.'' Randolph looked away from the two men for a moment and stared up at the map before he continued. ''You see, my wife, Martha, died giving birth to our daughter that night. I have never forgiven myself for not being at her side, even after all these years.''

Paul and Buck could see the mist forming in the man's eyes.

''Sir, we really don't have to go into this. We're going to get your daughter back. No matter—'' Stryker was cut off by the millionaire.

''No! No, Mr. Stryker, that has been the problem all along. I have never had the time to talk about my daughter. Time! My God. Where has all the time gone? I thought money could buy anything, but for a second time in my life I made a major mistake. Denise practically grew up with maids and servants caring for her. I hardly ever saw her in those early years, and when I did, I only allowed her time for a hug and a pat on the head; then, I would be gone again. I was so caught up in my own ambitions that I never took the time to notice the hurt in her eyes when I would leave. She was a beautiful child, so much like her mother.''

Buck was starting to get a little misty-eyed himself when he said, ''Mr. Randolph, you're really bein' pretty tough on yourself.''

''No, Mr. Buchanan, it was tougher on her. One day I turned around and my little girl was a woman. She had stopped the hugging long before that, and I hadn't even noticed the change. She attended three different colleges in two years and never graduated from any of them. College was boring so she quit and fell in with the jet set crowd. She'd spend a night in London, then be in Paris or Madrid the next night. She had unlimited funds and she knew it. I suppose she felt that as long as she stayed out of Daddy's hair it was going to be an unending party. It's been that way for the last three years.''

''My God,'' said Buck. ''A three-year bender. Hell, I wouldn't know where I was half the time.''

''She didn't either, Mr. Buchanan. That was why I had to start sending Mr. Novak's men with her. Of course, there were the constant French Romeos, Spanish playboys, and just about every kind of money-hungry sleaze in the world trying to marry her once they found out who she was. Novak made the suggestion and I went along with it.

They never interfered. She could have her fun, but they stepped in when some guy started getting serious.''

Stryker finished his drink, then asked, ''Why didn't you just cut her off at the purse strings?''

''Believe me, Mr. Novak suggested that on more than one occasion. But you see, money was all I had ever been able to give her. I couldn't bring myself to take away the very thing that had kept us apart all those years. So I let it go on.''

Both men could hear the heavy sadness of the words in the older man's voice. They were the words of a father who realized how much had been lost with the passing of time, and now wanted somehow to recover those lost years.

Buck asked, ''But why a refugee camp in Thailand?''

Stryker saw a beam of pride light up in the man's eyes as he answered. ''She saw a documentary about Na Pho on English television one night. Novak's men said she was overwhelmed by the show and wanted to go there to see if she and her friends could help. They all thought she was crazy. I suppose I wasn't much better. When Novak's men wired me about what she wanted to do, I told them it was fine and not to worry. I figured a week away from the parties and fine restaurants and she'd be out of there in a hurry. We were all wrong. She became completely involved in her work with the Catholic order at the camp. I received telegrams from her requesting money or various medical supplies. I even put on a special staff to handle those requests.''

''Sounds like the young lady was starting to get it together,'' said Stryker.

"She was, Mr. Stryker. I received a letter from her dated a few days ago. Not a wire, mind you, but a full four-page letter. That letter is the first one she's written me in over six years. I knew something was different when I read it. She didn't ask for money. All she wanted was for me to come to Na Pho. She wanted me to meet her new friends and see what she was doing. She just wanted us to spend some time together. At the end of the letter, she said she just wanted me to be proud of her."

Randolph's voice began to quiver with those words. Tears were clearly forming in his eyes as he tried to continue.

"I only . . . only wish that for . . . for once, I could have been there when my little girl . . . needed me. Now I may never get the chance to tell her how . . . how wrong I've been about so many things . . . and how much I love her."

"You're going to have that chance, Mr. Randolph. We're going to get her back. You have my word on that," said Stryker as he placed his hand on the man's shoulder.

"I know you will, son. I have to believe that. Please . . . please excuse me."

Both men watched as Randolph left the room. Buck looked down at the drink in his hand. "Boy, that's one guy that's tearing his guts out right now."

"You said it, buddy. The guy's got class and I've made a promise. We've got to make sure we pull this one off, Buck," said Stryker.

"I hear you, partner."

Richards and Novak joined them as they turned to the map.

"Any ideas, Stryker?" asked Novak.

"Yeah, I got a couple, but we'll wait to see what

Rick has for us. No sense in trying to second-guess on this one.'' Turning his attention to Richards, he asked, ''How many people did you say you had, Colonel?''

''Ten here and another twenty back in L.A.''

''Okay. I've got Buck, Doc and Pete. Hopefully Jake McKenna will hook up with us if we ever find him,'' said Stryker.

Novak stepped forward. ''You know I lost four damn good men at that camp. I plan to be in on this thing when it goes down.''

''It ain't gonna be no picnic, Mr. Novak,'' said Buck.

''Neither was the Tet offensive or storming the damn walls of the Citadel at Hue, Mr. Buchanan. I spent two long years in that shithole of a country and another three in Lebanon, which wasn't a hell of a lot better. I can handle it, if that's what's bothering you.''

Richards made a point of clearing his throat before he spoke. ''Mr. Novak, Paul Stryker will be in charge of the ground forces for this operation. If he wants you along, that's fine. If he doesn't, you're out.''

Novak started to object, but it wasn't necessary, as Stryker said, ''Hell, Novak, if you want to give them another shot at your ass, that's fine with me. I've got no objections.''

Novak smiled for the first time that afternoon. It was a smile that didn't go unnoticed by Buchanan. After he asked Stryker if he wanted another drink, he turned to Novak. ''Remember what they say, ol' boy, the third time's the charm.''

Novak's smile quickly faded. Walking up to the bar, Buck wondered why in the hell he'd said that.

He didn't have anything against the guy. It was just that Army people naturally loved screwing around with Marines. It seemed like the thing to do at the time. Any Marine who'd survived the Tet offensive at the Citadel was either awful lucky or damn good. Buck had a gut feeling that Novak wasn't the kind of guy to rely on luck.

Randolph came back into the study just as the phone rang. Everyone stopped talking, their eyes on the phone. The room was silent. Richards let the phone ring three times before answering.

"Yes, Operator, this is Erin Richards. Yes, thank you, I'll hold." The men in the room seemed to be drawn toward Richards like a magnet. Randolph stood next to the colonel, a look of anxiety on his face.

"Rick . . . Rick, can you hear me okay? Good. I think we should switch over to *Daniel* now."

Richards pressed the On switch at the top of the black box that was positioned next to the phone. He placed the receiver into the cradle of the scrambler code named Daniel. He turned on the speaker box so that those in the room could monitor the conversation.

"Rick, you still there?"

"Receiving you loud and clear, Erin. How you doing, Colonel?"

"Fine, Rick. Were your people able to come up with some answers for us?"

"Sure thing, Colonel, but it didn't come cheap. Two of my people were killed by the NVA before they got back across the Mekong."

"Sorry to hear that, Rick," said Richards, as the others in the room glanced nervously at each other.

"Yeah. It goes with the business, Erin."

Randolph leaned forward and spoke into the box, "Mr. Alley, this is Johnathan Randolph. I'm sorry about your two people. Rest assured that their families will be well taken care of from now on."

"Thank you, sir. It will be greatly appreciated. Erin, I sent seven of the boys across the river as soon as I got your call. Three made it back okay. Two were killed, and I still haven't heard from the other two. I can give you what I have up to this point."

"That'll be fine, Rick. Go ahead."

"We're dealing with a real nasty dude, Erin. Character's name is Phon Van Bao. He's the leader of a bunch of cutthroat Laotian bandits. Calls himself a colonel and receives weapons, ammo, and supplies from both the NVA and the Russians."

Stryker could see the look of confusion on Randolph's face at the references to the bandits, NVA, and Russians. He tried to clear it up for him. "You see, sir, the NVA and the Russians supply the firepower for these attacks against the Thai villages and border outposts. When a complaint is brought before the United Nations, Moscow and Hanoi throw their hands in the air and say, 'Hey, it's not us! It's those damn bandits.'"

A look of disbelief came into Randolph's eyes as he said, "But they provide the means for this death and destruction. They are responsible."

"Exactly, sir, but as far as the rest of the world is concerned their hands are clean. All very neat and tidy."

Randolph shook his head as they turned their attention back to the phone conversation.

"Rick, do you have a general area or location for this guy Bao's base of operations?"

"There are two areas we are sure of, Erin. Do you have a map handy?" Buck set his drink on the table, found a marker, and stepped in front of the map. "Yes we do, Rick. Go ahead."

"Okay, Erin, these are the two that we can confirm at the moment. There could be more, but judging from their size, I'd say these are two of his primaries. One is located three miles north of Mahaxia. It's a good bet that that's where they are right now. It's almost on a straight line from Na Pho and thirty miles inside Laos. Like I said, Erin, this guy is nobody's dummy. He doesn't stay in one place very long. He's got a second big base camp farther north, about fifty miles upcountry, place called Ban Nape. Afraid that's it as far as base sites go, Erin. I might have more for you when my other two boys get back in here. Till then, that's it on locations."

Buchanan circled the two locations on the map in red marker.

"Rick, this is Paul Stryker."

"Hey, Paul. Been a long time, ol' buddy. I was hoping the colonel would get you in on this. Is Buck with you?"

"You got it. I got a question for you. Any idea how large a force Bao has with him?"

"Wondered when somebody was going to ask that. Best we can tell right now, close to six hundred. How many folks you bringing with you?"

"Twenty-four—maybe twenty-five."

The casual manner in which Stryker had answered astonished Randolph. "Twenty-five men against six hundred!"

There was a pause on the end of the line before Alley asked, "Paul, are you bringing Jake McKenna with you?"

"Can't answer that right now, Rick. I sure as hell hope so."

"I'll be honest with you, Paul. Without Jake, you're going to have a mighty hard row to hoe, ol' buddy. Don't underestimate this guy. Bao's about as tough as they come, and that ragtag army of his is made up of some of the worse hardcases in Southeast Asia. They're all ex-soldiers and experienced jungle fighters, and brother, they're armed to the teeth."

"We figured as much, Rick. It's not going to be your average stroll in the park, that's for damn sure. Jake and his Meos could make the difference."

"How are we doing with the press blackout, Rick?" asked Richards.

"So far, so good, Colonel. The Thais have the place completely surrounded and locked down tight. Nobody in, nobody out. But who can say how long that will hold up."

"I agree, Rick. Gather whatever intell you can and have it ready when we arrive in country. It's going to be a horse race with the clock once we get our people on the ground."

"Okay, Erin. When can I expect you and the boys in Thailand?"

"If all goes as planned, we should be in Bangkok sometime within the next seventy-two hours. I'll give you an exact time; two hours out," said Richards.

"Sounds good, Erin. I'll have everything ready. You have anything more for me?"

"That's it, Rick. We'll see you in a few days."

"Roger, Colonel. Paul, it'll be good to see you and Buck again. Till then, so long."

Richards switched off the box and replaced the receiver back on the phone. Turning to Burford, he asked, "How are we doing with the passports, Mr. Burford?"

"I have them on the plane, Colonel. All we need to do now is type in the names and take the pictures. I have the equipment on board. Once you've made your personnel selections here, we can have their passports ready by the time we reach L.A."

Randolph asked, "Excuse me, gentlemen, but who is this man, Jake McKenna?"

"Ex-Special Forces Master Sergeant," said Stryker. "Won the Congressional Medal of Honor. Had four tours in the 'Nam and another four in Laos. Jake was the personal military advisor to General Vang Pho, who was the leader of the mountain tribes in Laos. The Meo were fighting the Communists in Southeast Asia before we even knew where the place was. Matter of fact, they never quit. Their admiration of Americans kind of hit the skids after we tucked in our tails and left them holding the bag. But Jake was kind of like a god to them. That's why we need him, sir. The Meo still have their weapons; and it's a damn good bet they would be willing to follow Jake anywhere he was willing to lead."

Novak had that look of doubt on his face again, but didn't say anything.

"Do we have any idea where he is?" asked York.

"Hell, Randy, we've turned this town upside—" The phone rang, cutting Stryker off.

Novak answered it. "Hello. Yes, I see. Okay, I'll tell him."

Hanging up the phone, Novak turned to Stryker. "That was Shannon. They've found your hero—he's in the drunk tank at the city jail."

Chapter 6

Colonel Kloskov sat at his desk studying the intelligence reports from the night before. One in particular caught his attention. At 0430 hours this morning, two Thai natives were shot and killed trying to evade a Pathet Lao patrol along the banks of the Mekong River. No identification papers or personnel documentation had been found on the bodies. There was no mention of weapons, and the men had been dressed in only shorts.

A patrol spotted the men on the bank and yelled a warning to halt. One broke into a run along the bank, while the other leaped into the Mekong and began swimming for the Thai side of the river. A quick burst of automatic weapons fire dropped the one on the bank. A steady aim and a single shot to the back of the head ended the swimmer's life. After they were confirmed dead, they were tossed back into the river.

Colonel Diem entered the office with two cups of coffee. Handing one to Kloskov, he asked, "What is the problem, Comrade? You seem worried."

Kloskov placed the file back on his desk as he smiled at Diem. "No, my friend. It is nothing. I was simply occupying my mind while waiting for a reply to our reports to Moscow and Hanoi.''

Diem made himself comfortable in an oversized stuffed chair that sat across from the desk. ''We should be receiving an answer soon.''

Both men had filed reports to their respective governments as soon as they had returned from Colonel Bao's base camp. Kloskov made sure that his report expressed Bao's utter contempt for the People's Party and especially for the Russians. His blatant denial of any knowledge of the raid on Na Pho or the whereabouts of the American prisoners was highlighted in the report. Diem did the same, but also worded his message in such a way as to leave his superiors wondering whether Colonel Bao was actually an asset or a threat to the Laos operation.

Diem took a sip of his coffee before asking, ''Comrade, would you think it possible that our superiors may have tired of this madman's continued troublemaking?''

''I can only hope that they realize the situation that Bao has placed us in at this time. Talks between the American President and the Premier are scheduled for later this month. This is a very bad time for us to face such embarrassment. You may be assured that this incident will be discussed at the meeting.''

Diem nodded in agreement as he took another sip of coffee. The door opened, and Kloskov's aide walked in with a message in his hand. Saluting smartly, the aide placed the message on the colonel's desk and left the room. Diem was on his feet and standing next to Kloskov as the Russian picked up the Teletype message and began to read.

011400067Z
SPASNW CMD
USSR/P1X2

Colonel Kloskov;
Laos Cmd/Vientiane

Situation as you have described is not acceptable to planned progress of area and People's Republic of Laos. Believe your assessment of elements involved in Na Pho affair creditable. However, new information has been received that one member of captured American party is daughter of American industrialist Johnathan Randolph, highly influential Capitalist who could be of enormous value to the state. Therefore, woman is top priority asset. Repeat—Top Priority! Follow all requests made by Colonel Bao until this woman is secured. Follow up with appropriate action to assure no such incidents can reoccur. Colonel Bao and his army of mercenaries have become a liability. Take whatever action you deem necessary.
END OF MESSAGE. . . . . . .

Kloskov glanced up at Diem. With a look of satisfaction he whispered, "Take appropriate action, Comrade. You realize what this means?"

Diem straightened himself up and grinned. "Yes, my friend, our fondest wish has been granted. Who is this Johnathan Randolph person that they speak of?"

"I am not sure. I know I have heard the name or read of him in the American papers. I would hazard a guess that this is the same woman that Bao was attempting to rape this morning when we arrived. We shall request more information on this person, and while we wait we can begin to formulate a plan of operation against Colonel Bao and his forces."

Diem seemed to be concentrating on something. There was a look of apprehension on his face.

"Is there a problem, Colonel Diem?"

"I have not yet received a reply from my command as to what action I should take. What if they should not agree with your superiors' evaluation and desire to continue the relationship with Colonel Bao and his forces in Laos?"

Kloskov leaned back in his chair and stared at the gray-haired man of fifty who had spent his entire life fighting wars. "My friend, do you really doubt that they will agree to this proposal?"

Before he could answer, the aide returned to the room. He held another message in his hand. Saluting again, he passed the message to Diem, then left. Diem read it silently to himself. As he finished, a broad smile came over his face. "You know the system well, Comrade. Except for my name on this piece of paper, the words are exactly the same."

"Of course, Diem. Our countries are brothers. We must work together if we are to achieve our goals. Come, we must prepare Colonel Bao a fitting reward for his outstanding service."

"Yes." Diem laughed. "Major Thieu will be especially happy to hear this good news."

As Kloskov closed the door behind them, a slight

breeze blew the papers from the top of his desk and onto the floor, all except one. It was an intell report about two Thai natives in another incident farther up the Mekong River. Shots had been fired, but the two had escaped safely across the river.

Major Lee Phong, Bao's second in command, moved around the camp giving the order to prepare to move out. As he approached the small confinement area in which the three nuns were being held, his eyes fixed on the young sister with raven-black hair and an attractive face. She wore an old sweatshirt and blue jeans. Kneeling by one of the elder sisters, Maria watched out of the corner of her eye as he approached. The two guards at the gate snapped to attention as he stopped in front of them and asked, "Are there any problems here?"

"N-no, Major Phong," stuttered one of the guards.

"Fine, open the gate. I wish to talk with one of the holy women."

Slinging his rifle, one of the men unlocked the padlock and swung the gate open for Phong. The major walked straight to Maria. Standing over her, he looked down and asked, "Is the old woman ill?"

There was no mistaking the contempt in her eyes as Maria stared up at the man and said, "What the hell do you care?"

Phong was momentarily taken aback by the straightforwardness of the remark. He found it hard to believe that this woman was a nun. Her dress and now her language did little to convince him that she was a member of a Catholic order.

"Why do you think I would not be concerned about a sister of God?" asked Phong.

"You cared damn little about Father Rogers or the other poor bastards at Na Pho. I believe that's a pretty good reason. You are nothing more than a cold-blooded killer and a cancer upon your own country."

"You are quick to judge those you know little about, young sister."

"Oh, I know you characters all right. You are no different than the vultures that lurk in the back alleys and doorways of New York. You feed on the weak and the helpless. What you cannot take, you destroy. No, there are those just like you all over the world, and one day you will be called to face judgment for what you have done."

Phong found this young woman exciting. She spoke as if he were the prisoner. There was a certain fire in her eyes and a bite in her words that he found admirable. If she feared her capturers, she hid it well. Kneeling down beside her, he placed his hand on the forehead of Sister Helen, the eldest member of the order. She had a fever and was beginning to show signs of breaking out in cold sweats.

"How long has she been this way?" asked Phong.

Maria watched the gentleness shown as he placed his hand on the woman's head. She heard the concern in his voice. He was a rather handsome man with a strong but caring face, and there was something about him that made him seem different from the others, a certain sense of kindness, a true sense of caring.

"It began about an hour ago."

Phong noticed how the old woman flinched as his knee touched her shoulder when he leaned over her. Carefully raising the sleeve of her shirt, he saw a deep gash at the very top of the shoulder. At the end of the cut there was a dark, almost black, spot.

"Oh, my God! She never said she was hurt. What is that black thing?" asked Maria.

Phong reached into the side cargo pocket of his jungle fatigues and pulled out a small knife. Opening to the smallest of the blades, he looked over at Maria and Sister Monica, who had just joined them. "You both must hold her very still. Do you understand?"

"What . . . what are you going to do?" asked Maria.

"Just do as I say. You will see," said Phong.

Monica looked into Maria's eyes, searching for an answer. Maria glanced away from her and at Phong, who waited patiently for them to follow his orders. For some reason she could not explain, Maria trusted this man. "Do as he says, Sister Monica."

Phong allowed a slight smile to appear at the corner of his mouth as he looked away from Maria and began his work. Edging the sharp, pointed end of the blade into the tail end of the wound, he worked the end of the knife under the black spot. Sister Helen's eyes shot open in pain as she struggled against the hands that held her down. Phong's words were soft and comforting as he said, "I am sorry, Sister, but this must be done. I will try to hurry."

Working over half of the length of the blade under the spot, Phong slowly twisted the blade a half-turn right, then back left. Keeping pressure applied downward on the blade, he withdrew it slowly. The two nuns watched in amazement as the small dot began to come out with the blade. The dot was not a dot at all, but rather the head of a black thorn over one inch long. Having worked a portion of it out, Phong removed the knife and gingerly gripped the exposed end of the thorn. He quickly pulled it out of the wound. A sigh of relief escaped Sister Helen's lips.

Holding the thorn between his fingers, he held it up. "It is the thorn of the chacoga palm. They are very hard and very infectious. She must have picked it up on the trek through the jungle during the night. I will send one of my medical people over to clean this up. He has experience with these things. She should be feeling better by the time we reach our new campsite tonight."

Phong stood and folded the knife, dropping it back into his pocket. Maria stood before him. Reaching out her hand to him, she said, "Thank you. . . . I'm sorry, I don't even know your name."

"Phong. Major Lee Phong."

"Major, then this really is an army. But I'm confused, Major. Are you Laotian army or Vietnamese? I see both here, but no standard uniform. You, yourself, are Vietnamese, are you not?"

Phong seemed almost embarrassed by the question as he looked through the wire at the odd collection of men that moved about the camp. They were a far cry from the crack North Vietnamese unit he had commanded against the American Marines and Army soldiers in Vietnam. True, he was a Vietnamese officer, or he had been. A drunken party after their victory in Saigon had led to an argument over a woman and a brawl had ensued between him and another officer. Sometime during the fight, a gun had appeared and shots had been fired. The other officer lay dead with Phong left holding the gun that had ended the man's life. The dead officer had come from a well-to-do family who had friends in high places. He had been arrested and ordered to stand trial for murder. The younger officers of the unit discovered that the trial was to be no more than a showcase of justice. The verdict had already been decided.

The night before the trial was to begin, they broke him out of jail and secretly smuggled him out of the country and into Laos. His young officers had followed Phong bravely for five long years, and the thought of such a man being put to death over a simple argument that had gotten out of hand was more than they could stand. Besides, the gun had been drawn by the dead man anyway. They had risked all to save their commander, but it was no less than he had done for them countless times in countless battles. They left him at the border with new clothes, food, and money. It was the best they could do. Their final farewell as he left them instilled a feeling of pride that even now, as he looked upon this sorry collection of soldiers around him, still remained. The Vietnamese takeover of Laos had driven him into the hills, where he had finally joined up with Colonel Bao. He had no great love for the man, but at least there was safety in numbers, and war was all that he knew.

How could he explain all this to the young

woman who now stood before him with her questions. He realized that he could not. "I suppose you could call us an army, Sister. You are right; I am Vietnamese."

Maria could sense a tone of discouragement in his voice. "Well, Major Phong, if you are not a Laotian unit nor a Vietnamese unit, what kind of army is this?"

"It is an army of liberation like no other, Sister."

"But who are you liberating?"

"Ourselves. We are liberating ourselves from the politics and overbearing authority that profit from war at the expense of the common soldier's suffering. We are finally taking for ourselves."

"But if you have no cause, no final objective or goal to achieve, where can such an army go?"

"To hell, Sister. . . . All the way to hell!" said Phong as he turned to walk away. Pausing a moment, he glanced back at her and said, "I will have the medic come at once. It has been a pleasure talking with you, Sister. Thank you."

He was gone before Maria could answer. She watched him make his way across the center of the camp and into Bao's tent. He seemed tired as he walked, as if the discussion had weighed heavily on him. Looking down at the thorn she still held in her hand, she tried to figure out what kind of man Major Lee Phong really was. She had thought she knew in the beginning, but now she found herself filled with doubt. A part of her knew that he liked her, yet another questioned if his kindness to her was only a lonely man wanting to talk with a woman. Whichever it was, she felt she now had a friend among the pack of wolves that surrounded them.

Sister Monica asked, "Didn't he say something about us leaving this place today?"

"Yes, Colonel Bao's men are already beginning to break camp. We must gather our things and be ready. I pray that Denise is all right. Maybe I can convince Major Phong to let her stay with us tonight."

Maria saw the small trail of tears making their way down Monica's face. Placing her hand on the frightened and depressed woman's arm, she said, "Remember what Father Rogers used to say, Sister. 'Keep the faith, and He shall not abandon thee.'"

"I know, Maria, but it seems as though we are totally alone here. It is as if the whole world is unaware of our plight. Surely someone must know what has happened. What is being done to help us? My God, what if they think we are dead and are doing nothing? We could . . . we could be here forever."

"Now, now, Monica, don't let your imagination run away with you. This ordeal will be over soon. These men have no desire to keep us with them. I am sure they are trying to figure a way to profit from our kidnapping. We must keep ourselves together and pray that it will be over soon. Now help me move Sister Helen back into the shade of the trees."

The calmness in Maria's voice and the logical manner in which she stated their position seemed to put Monica at ease. The older woman felt a spark of shame pass through her. Here she was, the older, but yet it was the younger one who had complete control of the situation. Maria might be young, and a little on the wild side as far as the order was concerned, but Monica was grateful that she was with her.

Chapter 7

The police sergeant glanced up from the mass of paperwork that was scattered across his desk as the four men came through the doors. Shannon spoke to Stryker and Buchanan for a moment, then left with Merrill. Stryker approached the desk and said to the sergeant, "Understand you have a friend of mine in there."

The overweight cop kept shuffling his papers around, and without looking up said, "If you got a friend in here, maybe you oughta find some new kind of friends."

"Yeah, you're probably right, but you see, I haven't got a lot of friends left. So if you don't mind, I'd like to see the one I do have."

The sergeant appeared irritated as he looked up at Stryker. "Okay, pal, just who is it we're talkin' about?"

"McKenna—Jake McKenna. He was brought in this afternoon."

"Oh yeah, the guy who tried to tear down the fuckin' Holiday Inn because he didn't like his room or some kind of shit. Don't know if he's outta the drunk tank yet. Gotta keep those juicers in there at least four hours, ya know."

Stryker glanced at Buck with a pained look in

his eyes. The colonel was right; Jake had hit rock bottom.

"Well look, could you check that out for us? We'd like to see about getting him out of here as soon as possible," said Stryker.

"Sure, no problem. But you better have a hell of a lot of money with you, pal. The damages to the hotel alone were fifteen hundred bucks. Then we've got the drunk and disorderly charge, an assault on police officers, damage to a police car—the son of a bitch tried to kick out the security screen in the back of the car. This boy thinks he's a regular Johnny Badass, don't he?"

Buck shook his head slowly as he listened to all the charges. The cop had it all wrong—this was a guy who just didn't give a shit anymore. Stryker said, "I don't really care what it costs. All I want to know is when I can see him and how long before I can get him out of here?"

The sergeant picked up the phone, punched a few numbers, then asked, "Hey Charlie, that drunk we brought in this afternoon dried out enough to have visitors? . . . Huh! . . . Yeah, okay, I'm sending a couple of guys back to see him. Give 'em 'bout ten minutes, then try and get the guy cleaned up enough to go before Judge Depee in an hour, okay? Right."

Replacing the phone, he stared up at Stryker. "Your boy got sick all over the place. He ain't smellin' real good, but if you wanta see him, go through that steel door there—last cell on the left all the way down."

Stryker nodded as he and Buck went through the door and down the row of cells. The odors of sweaty bodies and foul-smelling air filled their nos-

trils as they made their way to the last cell. A police officer was just opening the door to Jake's cell.
Neither Stryker nor Buchanan was prepared for the
sight of the man they saw huddled on a cot in the
corner. Jake McKenna looked like death warmed
over. The two-day growth of beard was just enough
to make his face appear dirty. His clothes were
ripped and torn from his battle with the police.
Spots of vomit clung to the front of his shirt and
covered the front of his wrinkled and worn pants.
There were cuts and bruises over his right eye. The
left side of his lip was split; a small trickle of blood
had made its way down his chin and onto his neck.
His eyes were sunken, hollow holes surrounded by
dark circles and swollen, red, puffy skin. Someone
had worked Jake over very well.

"Jesus, Paul," exclaimed Buck as he stared at
the huddled form in the corner.

A rage gripped Stryker. Grabbing the officer's
arm and with a threatening tone, he said, "Who
did that to him, Goddamn it?"

The young police officer stiffened as a glint of
fear crossed his eyes. "Hey, man, I just came on
duty. I don't know shit about it. They just told me
to get him cleaned up."

Buck stepped forward, took the pan of water and
washrag from the cop; then he walked into the cell
and knelt down by Jake. Stryker pulled on the cop's
arm lightly and backed him out of the cell.

"That's okay, kid. We'll take care of him now.
You just run on along, okay?"

"Sure . . . sure, man. I didn't want to mess with
that smelly shit anyway."

The cop closed the cell door and walked down
the hall. Buck was trying to get Jake to talk to him,

but was getting nowhere. Stryker sat down beside his old friend as Buck gently raised Jake's face and dabbed at the blood above his eye and around his mouth.

"Those motherfuckers beat the shit out of him, you know that don't you?" said Buck with bitterness.

"Yeah, I know, Buck. Some things about this fuckin' town won't ever change. One on one, these cops ain't shit. It takes five or six of the assholes to do something like this."

Stryker sat in silence for a few minutes; then he placed his hand under Jake's chin as he slowly moved the man's head around to face him. Jake's dark brown eyes seemed to stare off into space. It was as if the two visitors were not even in the room.

"Jake . . . Jake, it's Paul Stryker. Can you hear me, Jake?" No reply.

"Goddamnit, Jake. Snap out of this shit. I know you can hear me."

Jake's eyes showed no sign of recognition. Buck wet the rag again and pressed it softly against Jake's forehead. Stryker could see traces of water welling up in Buck's eyes as he stared at their old friend and comrade. They were both thinking of the fun-loving, hard-core Jake McKenna they remembered from the old days, with his booming voice of authority that had commanded respect from all who knew him. Jake had become a legend among the men of Special Forces. He was a real American hero. Now, here he sat in his own vomit, a beaten and broken man, not only physically but mentally. The sight tore at the hearts of both men.

"Jesus, Paul. We gotta get him out of here and quick."

"I know, Buck. You stay with him. I'm going to call Randolph. We'll just see how much pull the guy really has."

Stryker yelled to the kid at the end of the hall, who came down and let him out of the cell. In fifteen minutes, Stryker was back with Buck.

"What'd he say?"

"Told me to give him twenty minutes to work on it. Randolph said he'd see what he could do. Has Jake said anything?"

"Naw. Nothing, Paul. He just sits here staring at the wall. Maybe these assholes hit him one time too many."

"Maybe, Buck, but I don't think so. Jake's just kind of lost right now. If we can get him out of here and back to Sharon's place, we can clean him up and try to get some coffee and food down him. Maybe then a little sleep on some clean sheets and he'll come around. I've known this old war horse a lot of years. They don't come any tougher than this guy."

In the next thirty minutes they cleaned Jake up as best they could. They laid him down on the cot and waited. Stryker was about to make another call when the fat desk sergeant came lumbering down the hall and to the cell.

"You boys must know somebody with a lot of pull. I just got a call from the mayor's office and was told to let this piece of shit go. The charges have been dropped by the hotel."

"How 'bout the other charges?" asked Buck.

"Like I said, you boys must have a lot of grease in high places. Judge said we was droppin' them, too. Didn't set none too good with the officers that got punched out, but then, your friend there did 'fall down' a few times on the way back here. Clumsy fellow, ain't he?''

"Yeah," said Stryker. "You want to spare me the redneck bullshit and get this fucking door open so we can get out of here? The smell in this shithole just got a lot worse.''

The fat man opened the door as Stryker and Buck got on both sides of Jake and hoisted him to his feet. They practically had to carry him down the hall. Going out the front door they heard the sergeant yell, "You're wasting your time on that guy, boys. He'll be right back here in twenty-four hours. The guy's a loser.''

Placing Jake in the back seat of the car, they left the police parking lot and headed for Sharon Boyer's house. Within an hour, they had stripped Jake, stood him in the shower for a full twenty minutes and then put him to bed. Sharon was shocked at the sight of Jake. She thought of Charlotte. She found herself wishing Jake's wife were close by so she could call her to convince her to come to Jake's aid, but she didn't know where Charlotte was; and then again, maybe it was a bad idea.

Stryker hung up the phone and sat down at the kitchen table with Buck and Sharon.

Buck asked, "What'd the colonel have to say?"

Stryker took a sip of his coffee before answering. "He says we're going whether Jake's in or not. They're gathering the people together and taking off for California tonight. I told him to take Shannon and Merrill along with them, we'd be coming tomorrow afternoon. That dick, Novak, thinks it's a waste of time trying to get Jake back on his feet and into this deal. What's worse, Randolph's starting to lisen to the guy.''

Buck looked over at Sharon, then back down at his coffee cup before saying, ''You know, he may be right, Paul.''

Stryker slammed his fist down on the table, startling both Buck and Sharon. ''Damnit, Buck, now don't you start that shit. Why is it everybody wants to kick at Jake while he's down? What the hell ever happened to giving a guy another chance? Christ, Buck, that could just as well be one of us lying in there right now.''

''Because he doesn't fuckin' deserve one, you dumb ass!'' The three at the table turned to find Jake standing in the doorway. His words had caught them all by surprise.

Sharon jumped to her feet and helped Jake over to a chair at the table. He was still a little unsteady on his feet. ''Let me get you some coffee, Jake.''

His voice was shaky as he forced a smile and said, ''That'd be real nice, Sharon. Thank you, darlin'.''

''How you feeling, Jake?'' asked Stryker.

''Like I been rode hard and hung out wet. What the fuck you two degen'rates doing in Faggotville?''

''Well it was supposed to be a vacation, but it hasn't been workin' out too well. Not well at all,'' said Buck.

Jake reached across the table and shook hands with the two men as he said, ''You boys get me out?''

''Yeah, with a little help from some friends.''

Sharon set the coffee in front of Jake, then asked if he would like something to eat. Jake told her he'd pass on that for now. Just getting the coffee down was going to be hard enough.

"What the hell happened to you, Jake?" asked Stryker.

McKenna toyed with his cup for a moment, then looked across the table at both men. "Guess I just couldn't adjust to that fucking rat race those civilians run out there. They just weren't interested in trying new concepts or new ideas. Reckon I got off on the wrong foot with the boys down in Florida. I got the rep of being a troublemaker and a boat rocker. Hell, I didn't see it that way. There were some things that were just flat wrong, and I tried changing them. A lot of folks didn't like that. It was like hitting your head against a damn brick wall. One day they simply laid it on the line. Stay in your place and keep your mouth shut or you're outta here. Hell, if it hadn't been for Charlotte and the kids, I'd have told them to fuck off, but I couldn't do that. Charlotte was happier than I'd ever seen her before, Paul. We actually had a home that was ours. She could plant her roses and know that we'd still be there when they bloomed. You remember how she was about her roses, don't you, Paul?"

Stryker smiled as he thought of Charlotte McKenna, and nodded.

"It was everything she'd always wanted," continued Jake. "Hell, after dragging her around the world for twenty-two years, I figured she deserved to be happy for once. So, I shut up and tried to play the game. Guess I didn't do very well with it." Jake paused and took a sip of his coffee before he continued. "Started coming home at nights and just sitting in front of the TV. Not talking much, just drinking all the time. Got to where I hated to go in in the mornings. I don't exactly know when it started going to shit, Paul. It just did. I'd argue with Charlotte over the littlest things. I was always yelling at the kids and embarrassing them in front of their friends. Got so bad they stopped having the other kids over. 'Course, I was drinkin' so much all the time, I never really noticed it.''

Jake's voice trailed off for a moment. The others in the room stared down at their cups in silence. Jake wasn't drunk now, and listening to his own story, he was realizing just how bad it sounded. He forced down another shot of the coffee before starting again.

"Charlotte saw what all this was leading up to, but I wouldn't listen to her long enough to do anything about it. I was totally out of control. It was affecting my job and my home life, both, and it didn't get anything but worse as time went on. One night, in a drunken stupor, I hit my son. Hell, I didn't even remember doing it.''

"Jesus, Jake. What the hell was it? You couldn't work with these guys or what?'' asked Stryker.

"No, I couldn't, Paul. They didn't have that closeness we had in Special Forces—that all for one and one for all attitude. With them, it was promotions and back stabbing anybody you had to to get to the top. Real rat race, let me tell you.''

"Why didn't you talk it over with Charlotte, Jake? I'm sure she would have listened. You could've gotten another job or something,'' said Sharon.

"You're right of course, Sharon. I guess I'd let it go so long, it just didn't matter anymore. By then the bottle was making my decisions for me. As long as I had that bottle, I could handle anything. Before I knew it, I had driven Charlotte and the kids away from me. Came home one night, and she was gone. Didn't really blame her. Surprised she stayed as long as she did. Next came the business with the drug dealers. I blew the assholes away and almost went to prison for it. Needless to say, I didn't have a job with the law after that. Haven't done much of anything since then, either.''

Sharon went to the counter and returned with the coffeepot. There was silence as she refilled the cups and returned to her seat.

''What are you doing for money, Jake?'' asked Stryker.

''I kept a little of the retirement money. Sent Charlotte and the kids the rest of it. Sent her the money from the sale of the house and the cars, too. Hell, wasn't her fault I couldn't cut it out there.''

''Have you talked with her since then, Jake?'' asked Sharon.

''Not lately. She told me if I ever get it together to come see her. For some damn reason, the woman still loves me.''

Sharon patted the back of Jake's hand and winked at him. ''Of course she does, you big ox. All us girls are suckers for you SF fucks.''

Jake laughed for the first time.

''Nice talk for a young lady. Your dad would be turnin' you over his knee, he heard you talking like that.'' Playfully grabbing at her from across the table, he laughed. ''Hell, I might just do it myself.''

Sharon screamed jokingly, jumped up and ran to hide behind Stryker. ''You have to spank him first, Jake. He's the one who taught me to talk like that.''

Jake grinned. "I wouldn't doubt that." Looking across at Stryker and Buck, he asked, "Now, what the hell are you two doing here, really? I know you didn't come all the way back here just to get an over-the-hill drunk outta jail."

Pulling Sharon's arms from around his neck, Stryker smiled at Sharon and asked her if she would mind leaving them alone for a while.

"No problem, love," she replied, giving him a kiss on the cheek. "I've got to do the books at the club anyway. See you all later."

Waiting until the front door shut behind her, Stryker poured more coffee, then began. "Jake, Colonel Richards has a situation on his hands, and he needs some help. He's asked Buck and me to go along with him, but it's going to be a sticky deal, Jake, and we're going to need an edge."

Jake was suddenly aware of the fact that his hand was shaking as he tried to pick up his coffee cup. This was more coffee than he had drunk in three months. He was usually halfway through a bottle of Jack Daniel's by this time of the day. Right now his system was reminding him of that fact. The problem didn't go unnoticed by the two men across from him. Placing the cup down, Jake moved his hand away slowly and asked, "What kind of an edge are you talking about, Paul?"

Stryker was thinking of the colonel's words at the Sheraton earlier in the day. If Jake was brought in on this, then went out on a bender and talked to anybody, the entire operation would go down the tubes. Stryker studied the shaking hands and weatherworn face of his oldest friend before asking bluntly, "Jake, do you think you can stay sober long enough to work an operation with us, or are you too far gone to handle it?''

The straightforwardness of the question brought a shocked expression to Buck's face and one of hurt and anger to Jake's. The speed with which the big man came to his feet surprised even Stryker. Jake's big fist came across the table in a wide swoop and caught Stryker a glancing blow off the right temple, knocking him out of the chair. Buck jumped up just in time to catch a left cross square on the chin which sent him across the small confines of the kitchen and into the refrigerator. Stryker was trying to get to his feet as Jake came around the table and grabbed him by the front of his shirt. Jake flung him like a rag doll across the table and onto the floor again. Buck came at Jake with his right fist cocked back, but before he could throw the punch, Jake sidestepped him and slammed his fist into his gut, taking the air out of the big man. Jake finished him off with a chop to the back of the neck. Buck pitched forward onto the table and slid to the floor. He was out.

Paul Stryker wiped the blood from his lip as he came to his feet and yelled, "Okay, motherfucker, you wanta play; then by God we'll play."

A wide grin came over Jake's face. He suddenly seemed twenty years younger as he laughed. "Hell, boy, you ain't never seen the day you could take this old man."

Stryker ducked a barnyard left thrown by Jake, then he stepped in close and swung a left of his own that caught Jake just below the right eye and sent him barreling into the full-length planter that separated the kitchen from the living room. Jake's weight crumpled the lightweight wood that held the flowers and plants, spilling dirt, plants, and himself onto the living room carpet.

"Damn, kid, if that's the best you got, you had better check into an old-age home," said Jake as he pulled himself up onto his knees smiling. Blood flowed down the left side of his chin.

Stryker bellowed, "We haven't even started yet, you old fuck!" Leaping through the shattered planter, Stryker fell on top of Jake. The two men rolled across the floor, each trying to gain the advantage. Stryker blocked a knee to his groin and slammed an elbow into Jake's nose. The blow brought a splattering of blood that covered the wall behind them. Jake spit, then brought both hands up, palms open, and popped Stryker on each side of his head about the ears. The pain brought a scream from Stryker. "Son of a bitch!"

Jake was smiling as he said, "Didn't know you knew my mother, dickhead!"

The battle raged from the front room down the hall, in and out of one of the bedrooms, and back into the living room. The cut over Jake's right eye that had been received courtesy of the Fayetteville police was bleeding again, so were his nose and lips. Stryker had a split lip and a cut above his nose. Both men were on the verge of exhaustion as they faced each other on their knees exchanging blow for blow. Buck finally came around and sat in the middle of the shattered planter with a beer in his hand watching the two men beat hell out of each other. He'd had enough of this crap.

Jake struggled to bring his arm up to block a blow from Stryker, but his arm felt like it weighed a ton. The blow glanced off his shoulder and sent him back against the recliner that sat against the wall.

"You had enough, you hardheaded shit?" asked Stryker, panting heavily.

Pulling himself halfway up against the chair, Jake grinned. "Reckon you got me, kid." Raising his hand to Stryker he said, "Help an old man up, will you?"

Stryker crawled forward and reached out his hand. Jake's foot shot out, catching him on the chin and flipping him backwards into the coffee table.

"Damn, Stryker, thought I taught you better than that. You don't trust anybody—ever! Ain't that right, Buck?"

Buck raised his beer in a toast as he said, "That's what you always told us, Jake."

Jake walked over and helped Stryker to the kitchen table. Pulling another beer from the ice-box, he opened it and set it in front of Stryker.

"Now you were askin' if I thought I could hang with you hotshots. Well, I think I can. Even if I am a fuckin' drunk, that don't mean I like hearing it from my friends. Now, if you need some help you just say so, you don't get personal, okay? So, now that we got shit out of the way . . . how much does the job pay? Where is it? And when are we leaving?"

Chapter 8

Colonel Kloskov received the intelligence profile on Johnathan Randolph and Randolph Industries. Double agents in the Na Pho refugee camp confirmed that one of the women taken by the bandits was Denise Randolph. Headquarters in Moscow wanted the girl in Kloskov's hands as soon as possible. He was not to take any action that could endanger the girl's life. Once she was safely out of the area, the colonel could then deal with Bao.

At first, Kloskov had not seen the importance of rescuing this American woman. However, after reading the file, he could understand his superiors' orders and their concern for this girl's safety.

Randolph Industries held major oil concessions in Israel as well as controlling interest in a large part of South Africa's mining complex. By holding Randolph's daughter, they might be able to influence oil production in Israel as well as disrupt the economy and labor force inside South Africa. This would force the closing of the mines and the withdrawing of all assets from South African banks.

These were only a few of the possibilities. With a man as powerful as Randolph, the options were numerous. First, they had to have the girl.

Colonel Diem had already sent messages to three

NVA companies that were located in the general vicinity of Xieng Khouang Valley. They were to mass those companies outside the village of Ban Namay and await his arrival for further instructions. Major Thieu completed the organization and loading of the required convoy. The trucks sat lined along the road with their canvas-covered beds filled with the weapons and ammunition that had been requested by Colonel Bao. Colonel Kloskov's jeep sat in front of his headquarters. In the rear was a steel box. In this box was $100,000 in gold. Kloskov had no intention of letting Bao get his hands on one ounce of that gold. Once the girl was out of danger, he would recover the gold and send it back to Vientiane along with the head of the bandit leader.

Colonel Diem and Major Thieu came into the office just as the Russian advisor completed a final message to be sent to Moscow. They were ready to begin their trip to the valley and the final confrontation with Colonel Bao. Thieu had brought a bottle of wine with him. Pouring three glasses, he raised his in a toast. "To our two great countries and victory."

The colonel repeated the words. All three drained their glasses and set them on the desk. Kloskov said, "Come, gentlemen. Within three days' time, we shall present Colonel Phon Van Bao with his just reward."

Major Phong was as good as his word. His medic had attended to Sister Helen and had given her a shot of morphine for the pain. She was resting quietly now. A litter was fashioned from two poles and ponchos snapped together to carry her as they moved out of the base camp. Maria sent a message back with the medic for Major Phong. She was requesting that Denise be allowed to travel with them. Phong took the matter before Bao, who objected at first. However, the major convinced him that it was better to keep the prisoners all together than to have them strung out throughout the column.

Denise was provided a set of oversized jungle fatigues to replace her torn clothing. Hugging Maria and Sister Monica, she showed a look of concern when she saw Helen lying on the litter with her eyes closed. Maria reassured her, "Do not worry, Denise. She is only sleeping. Thanks to an unexpected friend. She will be fine by morning."

"A friend?" asked Denise.

"Yes," said Maria. "At least I like to think he is a friend. He's not like the others. There's something about his eyes and the way he talks. It was he who was responsible for getting you away from that god-awful Bao and back with us."

Denise seemed confused by Maria's words; however, she was not about to question the reasons behind them. She was among her friends again and away from the clutches of that madman Bao. That was all that mattered. She asked, "Do you have any idea where they are taking us?"

"A place called the Khouang Valley, I think," said Maria.

"I wonder why," said Denise.

"I'm not really sure, honey, but I get the feeling it has something to do with those three men who were here yesterday. Two of them were NVA officers, and I believe the third was German or Russian; I don't know."

Denise's eye lit up for a moment as she said, "He was a Russian. Bao said something about a Russian was going to save us or something like that. God, this is all so confusing. Do you think anyone is looking for us yet, Maria?"

Maria bent down and covered Sister Helen with a poncho as two of the bandits came over to carry the litter. Placing her arm around Denise, she hugged her gently as she answered. "Honey, I don't know what else is going on in the world, but I'm willing to bet you that somewhere out there somebody is working on getting us out of this mess. We've just got to stick together and pray to God that it will be over soon."

Denise wiped the beginning of a tear from her eyes as she hugged Maria. "Thank you, Maria."

"For what?"

"Oh, just for being here—and for being you."

Maria smiled. No words were necessary as the two women held hands and walked out the gate behind the litter. Colonel Bao's army was on the move. The bandit leader smiled to himself as he walked along thinking of how he was going to spend his gold. He had made up his mind during the night that this was going to be his last operation in Laos—his last operation anywhere. With the gold he would receive for the Americans, he was going to leave the country. His army could fend for itself. He would head for Paris and a life of ease. He owed that to himself.

Stryker, McKenna, and Buchanan arrived in L.A. the following morning. They were met at the airport by Novak and Burford. Novak commented about the black eyes that both Stryker and Jake were sporting. Paul Stryker told him they had gone to one too many parties before leaving Fayetteville. Novak tried the same coolness on Jake that he had used on Stryker and Buck at their first introduction, but Jake wasn't buying it. Jake McKenna told Novak that he had yet to find a fucking thing that he liked about a Marine. Novak was visibly angered by the comment as they loaded into the van that would take them to Randolph Industries. Sliding behind the steering wheel, Novak remarked, "I would have expected more from a Medal of Honor winner, Mr. McKenna, but then, you don't often find 'heroes' of any type in jail."

McKenna leaned back in the seat and lit a cigarette before asking Stryker, "This guy always been a dick, or did you boys turn him into one with your sweet personalities?"

"Nope, Jake, the boy is a self-made man. Ain't that right, Mr. Novak?" asked Buck.

Novak gripped the steering wheel so tightly that his knuckles turned white. He bit at his lower lip to keep from saying anything. Novak had strict orders from Randolph. There would be no trouble between his security people and the team. The first incident and he would be fired, that simple. With that thought fresh on his mind, Novak held in the urge to pull the van off to the side of the road and take these overconfident Green Berets on one at a time. He wanted to show them how effective one Marine could be. True, they might whip his ass, but brother, they would know they had been in a fight when the dust settled. That was what he really wanted to do, but this was not the time or the place. He would wait. Somewhere during this operation he was going to get his chance; then he'd see who talked shit.

It was nine in the morning when they reached the Randolph Building. Shannon, Merrill, and the others had already had their passports made. Colonel Richards and Randy York were glad to see the new arrivals, but obviously concerned at their rather beleaguered appearence. Stryker still stuck with his earlier story: the cuts, bruises, and black eyes were no more than the results of a last-minute brawl that had happened at a party. Richards wasn't buying that story, but there wasn't time to debate the issue. He wanted the team on the airplane and on their way by twelve noon. Time was not a commodity that they had a lot of. Therefore, the reunion was short and sweet. The aircraft was a chartered 747 and was already standing by. Richards received another call from Rick Alley. The Thais reported two men had escaped from Na Pho, and both were believed to be Communist double agents. The Thai government would not be able to keep the incident a secret much longer. It was imperative that Richards be in Thailand by tonight. The colonel confirmed that they would be.

By 11:30 A.M. they were aboard the chartered aircraft. Jake sat next to Stryker. Fastening his seat belt, he grinned and said, "Just like old times, huh, kid?"

Stryker saw Jake's hands trembling as the man fumbled with the belt. Jake hadn't had a drink in the last forty-eight hours, and it was beginning to show. Stryker wondered how long the man would be able to hold out. He pushed the question to the back of his mind as he grinned at his old team sergeant and winked. "You got that right, Jake.

Once more into the breach and all that Hollywood shit.''

Both men relaxed in their seats as the big jet lifted off the runway and climbed for altitude. In fourteen hours they would be in Thailand. Within twenty-four hours, they would be back in a hell that they knew all too well. A hell filled with steaming jungle, snakes, and men who would want only to kill them. It was something they understood. It was something they were good at.

Paul Stryker propped a pillow up against the small window next to his seat and slept soundly. He was dreaming of his last few hours with Sharon, the moments of laughter, of crying, of tender touches and whispered words of love.

She was asleep when he left. He had stood silently in the doorway taking in a last vision of her as she lay cuddled next to his vacant pillow. It was a picture he wanted burned in his memory. Her long hair spread over the pillowcase, its golden color a thing of beauty against the crisp whiteness of the sheets. The innocent little-girl look on her face as she slept. It was a look of perfect contentment. He'd told her how much he loved her. The words brought tears to her eyes, tears of joy. They were words she had longed to hear and words she had not heard for so long. He had repeated them to her until she had drifted off into a blissful sleep. Before leaving, he wrote ''I Love You'' on a piece of paper and then placed it on the kitchen table next to a small jewelry box that contained an engagement ring. Paul Stryker had made a commitment.

Jake McKenna eased himself out of his seat so

as not to wake Stryker. Moving to the rear of the airplane, he stepped into the bathroom. When he came back out, Johnathan Randolph was standing in the small kitchen area pouring a cup of coffee. "Ah, Mr. McKenna, would you like some coffee?"

"Yes, I would. Thank you."

Randolph opened an overhead cabinet and removed another cup. Jake felt his stomach tighten. Sitting in wire racks along the inside of the cabinet were rows and rows of the small liquor bottles used by the airlines. Jake couldn't remember when he had gone this long without a drink. Randolph handed Jake the cup of coffee as he asked, "Do you have any children, Mr. McKenna?"

Jake was grateful for the question. It took his mind off the bottles in the cabinet. "Yes sir, two, a son seventeen and a daughter fifteen."

"A son and a daughter. Ah yes, my Martha and I used to say that that would be the perfect family. One boy, one girl. She would have liked that. Where are they, Mr. McKenna?"

Jake leaned back against the sink as he said, "Mr. Randolph, since we're gonna be working pretty close together for the next few days, I'd really rather you called me Jake."

"Of course, Mr. McKen—I mean, of course, Jake."

"Thank you, sir. Don't mind tellin' you, hasn't been anybody called me Mister in a long time. To answer your question, the kids are with their mother in Oklahoma."

"Oklahoma. Big oil country out that way. Understand the state's been having a hard time lately.

Oil prices being what they are these days,'' said Randolph as he sipped his coffee.

"I wouldn't know. I haven't been there in a while."

Randolph thought for a moment he had misunderstood what Jake had said earlier.

"Oh, I thought you had been—"

"No, sir, my wife left me. Took the kids with her when she went. I haven't seen them or Oklahoma in quite a spell."

"I'm . . . I'm sorry, Mr. . . . Jake. I didn't know."

This discussion was not doing a lot to suppress Jake's desire for a drink.

"Hell, don't be sorry, sir. Smartest thing my wife ever did. Now, if you'll excuse me." Jake reached into the cabinet, grabbed a small bottle of Jack Daniel's and opened it. Pouring it into his coffee, he went back down the aisle. Finding a section where he could be alone, he sat and sipped his coffee. The steady hum of the engines were almost in rhythm with his thoughts. Staring out into the blackness beyond the window, he thought of Charlotte and the kids. Where were they now? What were they doing? Were they thinking of him? Paul had said this job was going to be a big one. They could write their own ticket. Money was no object. Maybe, just maybe, after this was all over, he could check himself into one of those alcohol treatment centers. He'd be able to afford the best in the country. Once he was straight, he could call her. Yeah, that's what he'd do. But for now, he needed this drink. Something inside himself told him he always would. . . .

Chapter 9

Rick Alley met the plane with transportation to take the team to a safe house outside Bangkok. After backslapping and handshakes had been exchanged all around, the group loaded into the vans and left the airport. Stryker, McKenna, and Richards sat in the back of the lead van. Rick was giving them an update.

"Some really weird shit going on out there, Colonel. My two missing men showed up a few hours ago. One of them was in Vientiane yesterday. He reported a large convoy was being put together by the NVA and the Pathet Lao. The trucks were loaded with weapons and ammo. He overheard one of the soldiers talking about the village of Ban Namay and the Plain of Jars."

Richards asked, "You think this convoy has any connection with Bao and the Randolph girl, Rick?"

"That's just it, Erin, I'm not sure. It seems damn funny that a convoy that size would have any connection with Ban Namay. That place is nothing more than a small village in an out-of-the-way place. There are no military installations or bases of any kind out there."

"How about the Plain of Jars, Rick?" asked McKenna.

"Well, Jake, they've a few outposts up around there, but the main forces are headquartered in the major cities off the plain."

Stryker thought about what Rick had said, then asked, "Rick, do your contacts in the agency have any information about planned offensives by the NVA or the Pathet Lao?"

"Nothing, Paul. Hell, they haven't mounted a large-scale offensive against anybody in over two years. Matter of fact, it's been pretty damn quiet around here. That's another thing. My boys tell me whatever is going on must be some pretty hot shit because Colonel Van Diem, the NVA commander, and Colonel Kloskov, his Russian advisor, are going out with the troops."

McKenna looked over at Stryker as he said, "You thinking the same thing I am?"

"Sure enough, Jake."

Richards and Alley waited for one of the two men to enlighten them. Richards leaned forward as he said, "I take it you two already have this thing figured out."

Jake lit a cigarette before he replied. "It's a shot in the dark, Colonel, but you have a larger than usual convoy of weapons and ammo headed for a place that has no military bases or large concentration of troops. There are no offensive operations going on anywhere in the country. Ban Namay is less than ten miles from the Plain of Jars. Rick, you remember the site we picked for the peace negotiations between General Phao, the Meo tribes, and the Communists?"

"Sure, Jake, the Plain of Jars."

"You remember why we picked that particular location?"

Alley thought for a moment, then answered. "Hell, yes, we didn't trust the Commie bastards to honor their part of the deal. The plain is flat enough that we could spot anyone amassing troops. You even put a team on Phou Bia, the highest damn mountain in Laos, just south of the plain. They could see for miles in all directions. Any wrongdoing going on, they were to call us on the radio."

Jake took a long drag on his cigarette as he kept his eyes on Rick. McKenna knew it wouldn't take the old-time CIA veteran long to figure it out. He was right.

Alley sat straight up. A grin worked its way across his face.

"Goddamn! That asshole Bao is trading the women for the weapons and the deal's going down on the Plain of Jars because he doesn't trust the Pathet Lao or NVA any more than we did back then, right?"

"You got it, Rick. Like I said, it's just a shot in the dark, but if I'm right, it could save us a hell of a lot of time."

Richards smiled at Stryker as he said, "Thanks, Paul."

"For what, sir?"

"For not listening to me, and for bringing Jake along."

"No problem, sir," said Stryker as he sat back in the seat and stared out the window. Stryker hid the uneasiness he'd felt when he saw the small bottles of whiskey in the overnight bag that lay at Jake's feet. The man had proven what an asset he could be to this operation. But then, he was sober, too. Stryker was a man torn between respect and love for an old friend and a deep concern for the lives of the men who were about to go into hell with him. His life and the lives of the others were going to depend totally on Jake McKenna. There had been a time when there would have been no need for that doubt, but the bottles in that bag had changed all that. Could they depend on Jake when the chips were down? That was the haunting question that ate away at Paul Stryker as he watched the lush colors of the Thailand countryside glide by his window. He had no positive answer for his question. Only time would tell—and yet, that was a luxury they didn't have.

The sweltering heat of the day's march had left the women exhausted. Major Phong had dropped back in the column several times to check on Sister Helen. He and Maria had exchanged glances, but never spoke.

Denise tried to pull her broken comb through her matted hair but with little success. In her frustration she threw the comb away. Maria came over and sat beside her.

"It doesn't look bad, really."

Denise ran her hand over her head. "Thanks, but I know better. How is Helen doing?"

"Much better. There is still some soreness in her shoulder, but I'm sure that it will be gone by tomorrow."

"Tomorrow." Denise sighed. "I wonder how many more tomorrows there will be for us?"

Maria lowered her head to her knees. She could smell the sweat from her own body that had soaked her clothes and left white, salty stains around the underarms of her shirt. She was so tired. She couldn't think of tomorrow. Tomorrow would bring more heat and more walking. Walking to a place she'd never heard of, for reasons she didn't know. The slums of New York suddenly didn't seem so bad. She had to stop thinking this way. Too many people were depending on her, Denise for one. She wasn't from the streets. How could she be expected to deal with this kind of hardship, to accept things for the way they were, with no hope of changing them. She had to stay strong for Sister Monica's sake as well. For although she was strong in faith, the older sister was weak in her ability to deal with reality. Stark reality now threatened to shake that faith. No, Maria couldn't allow herself to feel self-pity for her plight. If she came apart, so would the others.

"Maria, are you all right?" asked Denise as she gently placed her hand on Maria's shoulder. Her head still down, Maria reached up and covered Denise's hand with her own.

"Yes, I'm fine. I'm just a little tired, that's all. You need to get some sleep. I'm sure we will be moving again at daylight."

Denise gave her a hug as she said, "You're right. You get some rest, too, okay?"

Maria patted her hand, then stood and covered Denise with a poncho to ward off the cool air that sweeps over the Laotian mountains at night. The young girl had already lapsed into a sound sleep as Maria turned to leave. Stretching her tired, worn muscles, Maria made her way through the darkness toward the litter to make one last check on Sister Helen. A huge hand clamped over her mouth before she had a chance to scream. When she tried, nothing came out but a muffled sound. Another pair of hands grabbed her waist, and she was pulled into the thickness of the jungle. She tried to kick, but that only brought a hard slap to the face. The blow almost knocked her unconscious.

The stinking smell of sweat seemed to cover her face. The object in her mouth tasted salty. It was a sweaty bandanna from the neck of one of the bandits. Her T-shirt was pushed up as rough hands pawed at her bare breasts. Others roamed between her outspread legs. The two men spoke in excited whispers. Maria could not understand what they were saying, but as one stood and pulled his pants down she knew language was not important.

The man dropped down on top of her. Fumbling awkwardly in the dark, he finally achieved his goal and pushed forward with all his weight as he drove himself into her. Pain shot through her entire body as the man rocked wildly back and forth on top of her, his breathing coming in short gasps as he continued slamming his entire length all the way in, then brought himself almost all the way out, only to slam forward harder and harder each time. Maria struggled to place her mind somewhere else, in another time and another place, but the smell of the animal who was violating her was so strong that even that did no good. Harder and harder, faster and faster, and finally he heaved one final time with all his might and collapsed on her bare chest, his breathing heavy and labored.

The other bandit began pulling at the man on top of her in an effort to get him out of the way. Maria lay perfectly still. There was nothing she could do. Finally pushing his friend off of her, the second man reached forward and squeezed her breasts before lowering himself onto her. She felt

him enter her. She closed her eyes. She only
wanted him to hurry and get it over with.

A sudden warmth began to flow along her neck.
My God, the man was drooling all over her. No
. . . that couldn't be it. There was too much of it.
Opening her eyes, she tried to scream through the
confines of the stinking rag in her mouth. Above
her stood Major Phong holding the rapist by the
hair, tilting his head back. A long, deep gash ran
across his throat. Bright red blood gushed forth
from the massive wound. The warm, lifegiving
fluid spewed forth onto Maria's bare chest and
around her neck. She shut her eyes again.

Gentle hands slowly and carefully undid the gag
in her mouth as Phong spoke to her softly. "I am
sorry I did not get here sooner. Are you seriously
hurt?"

Maria couldn't answer. She shook her head no.
Phong turned and spoke with one of the men who
stood behind him. The man removed his fatigue
shirt and handed it to the major. Placing his hand
under her head, Phong raised her up and covered
her nakedness with the shirt. She stared into his
eyes for a fleeting moment. She saw the hurt there.
Looking away from him, she saw the first man who
had raped her standing to the left. One of Phong's
men had a rifle pressed against the man's back.

Phong helped her to her feet. There was a sharp
pain in her abdomen. It had been more than seven
years since she had been with a man. The pain
would disappear faster than the memory of what
had caused it. Denise was suddenly beside her.
Taking her by the arm, she lead Maria out of the
jungle and back into the campsite. Colonel Bao
met them as they emerged. Phong took him aside

and explained what had happened. Bao moved in front of the rapist and slapped him savagely across the face, knocking him to the ground. Orders were given to tie the man to a tree and keep him under guard for the remainder of the night.

Denise was given a canteen of water by one of the soldiers. Tearing a piece of cloth from her shirt, she poured the water over it and slowly cleaned the blood from Maria's body. When she had finished, she laid her friend back and covered her with a poncho. Denise sat, holding Maria's hand, until the young girl from New York was sound asleep; then she went back to her own sleeping area to get her poncho so she could remain close to Maria for the rest of the night.

Phong stood silently by a tree watching Denise approach. She could hear his honest concern as he asked, "How is she?"

"Sleeping."

"I am . . . I am sorry that this has happened."

Denise felt a sudden surge of anger streak through her. "Then why don't you end this, and let us go before it happens again."

Phong could understand her anger. It was no stronger than his own. "I cannot do that. You shall all be free soon. I will place my personal guards to watch over you for the remainder of our journey. Again, I am sorry."

Denise watched the major walk into the darkness. Picking up her poncho, she went to where Maria was sleeping and placed the cloth on the ground next to her. Lying down, Denise pulled the cover over herself and whispered, "I like your friend, Maria."

At first light, two of Phong's men came to

awaken the sleeping women. Maria was feeling sore, but able to travel. She asked that the other sisters not be told of what had happened to her. Denise agreed. Folding their ponchos and gathering their few belongings, they joined the column of soldiers that was beginning to form up around the campfire.

Sister Monica screamed and pointed in the direction of the trees to her right, quickly turning her head away from the gruesome sight.

Hanging from one of the outstretched limbs were the bodies of Maria's attackers. The men were stripped naked. The man Phong had killed hung upside down by his feet. His body was an ashen gray from the lack of blood, which had formed a pool below him. The second was hung by the neck. The only visible wound on his body was in the groin area. His private parts had been cut from his body and nailed to the tree.

Maria stared at the bodies for a long moment, but found it hard to feel pity for either of these men. The sign of the cross she made as they walked past the bodies was no more than a reflex action. She was sure that Father Rogers would have understood.

Chapter 10

Rick Alley acquired a large stucco house ten miles outside of Bangkok for their initial base of operations. It was situated in the center of an old French rubber plantation, which made securing the area simple but effective. Located three hundred yards beyond the house was an old airstrip that hadn't been used for years. Rick already had people clearing the overgrown grass and filling in the holes in the hard-packed clay that formed the runway. As they pulled up in front of the house, four Thai servants came down the front steps and helped remove the luggage. Stryker questioningly glanced in Alley's direction.

"Don't worry, Paul, they're my wife's brothers. Hell, I had to get 'em some kind of job. I already have three others working in my club. We can trust them if that's what you're worrying about."

Jake laughed as he said, "Hell, Paul, if a guy can't trust his own relatives, then who can he trust?"

Richards moved to the top of the steps. Looking out over the group, he asked for their attention. "Gentlemen, I know everyone is tired from our long trip, but time is a factor in this operation. I would like you to take thirty minutes to get yourselves squared away, then meet me downstairs for an operations briefing. So let's move it.''

Randolph and Burford wearily made their way up the steps. The heat of the night had both men sweating heavily. They discarded their ties and undid the buttons at the top of their shirts. Novak, on the other hand, did not appear to be bothered by the heat. Stryker was glad to see that. If the man was determined to go with them, he was going to have to hold his own. They were going to be moving fast once they were on the ground, and if the guy couldn't keep up, then it was going to cost them valuable time.

Jake McKenna dumped his clothes on the bed in his room. Picking up two of the small bottles of Jack Daniel's, he twisted off the caps and downed them both. He had wanted to do that in the van, but figured it would only worry the colonel and Stryker.

Once all the members of the team were assembled in the large patio area at the back of the house, Richards said, ''Gentlemen, as of this moment, this unit is operational.''

Turning to the maps and charts that York and Bobby Joe had placed against the wall, he continued. ''The operation will consist of four elements. The Headquarters and Control Element will be under the control of Major York, Mr. Alley, and me. This element will be known as Wolf Pack. Sergeant McKenna has been designated Lobo. Sergeant Stryker will be Lobo One and Sergeant Buchanan's group will be Lobo Two. Gentlemen, since time is pressing, we are going to skip the formal bullshit and go straight to the situation. Randolph's daughter and three American nuns have been kidnaped by a Laotian bandit named Phon Van Bao. He calls himself a colonel, and he has an army of over six hundred strong. We intend to go across the Mekong, kick this guy's ass and bring those four women home.''

This brought a cheer from the younger members of the unit.

''Enjoy yourselves now, boys. This is not going to be all that easy. We believe that Bao intends to exchange the women for a shipment of arms and ammo on the Plain of Jars sometime within the next forty-eight to seventy-two hours. If Bao should discover that one of his prisoners is Mr. Randolph's daughter before that exchange, you can bet he's going to hide her away and try to sell her to the highest bidder. If that happens, we'll never find her.''

Novak asked, ''I take it Bao is making this trade with the Laotians. Is that correct?''

''Yes, Mr. Novak, the Pathet Lao and the NVA.''

''So in other words, we not only have Bao and six hundred bandits to deal with, but who knows how many Laotians and NVA. I'm sorry, Mr. Richards, but even I, in my limited knowledge as a Marine, can count! Against those odds, it can't be done, not even by twenty Marines.''

Although Novak had been the one to say it, Richards could see the look of doubt on the faces of Randolph and Burford. Even some of the younger volunteers hesitated to challenge Novak's statement.

Jake McKenna spoke. ''Novak, you got the numbers wrong. It's not gonna be just twenty of us against a rucksack full of them. That's why I'm here. Now if you'll just let the colonel finish, I'm sure even you'll be able to figure it out.''

Novak had reached the breaking point in dealing with these overbearing Green Berets. It was time they realized he wasn't going to take any more shit from them. If Randolph didn't like it, fuck him, too.

"McKenna, you may have been some hotshot stud in your day, but even with that CMH you're nothing more than an over-the-hill drunk these overrated assholes feel sorry for. Twenty-four hours without a bottle and you'll be out of the goddamn game. You couldn't organize your way out of a fucking bar!''

Everyone stood in shocked silence at Novak's statement. Jake was the first to react. Screaming at the top of his lungs, he rushed across the patio and leaped on Novak. Both men went down hard on the concrete floor. Randolph was yelling for someone to break it up. Burford moved quickly back inside and watched from the double French doors that led to the patio. York started forward, but Richards grabbed his arm. It was best they got it settled now. Stryker waved off the others. Rick Alley shook his head and walked back inside to fix himself a drink.

Jake rolled over on top of Novak and swung a vicious left hook that caught the man square on the right cheek. Novak's right leg came up. His knee hit Jake in the middle of the back and sent him sailing forward off of Novak. Shaking his head slightly, Novak took the offensive. He charged straight at Jake as the man tried to pull himself up off his knees. Jake dodged the attack and swung a right that caught Novak in the midsection. The crowd around them heard the heavy rush of air that exited Novak's body because of the blow.

Jake gained his feet and waited for Novak to get up as he said, "Not bad for an over-the-hill drunk, huh, kid?"

While Novak was still gasping for breath, he came at Jake with both hands swinging. Jake blocked one, but the other got inside and landed above his right eye, stunning him for a moment. That was all Novak needed. Spinning on his left heel, he kicked his right leg straight out. His foot nailed Jake square in the chest and sent him flying backwards through the air and into the solid stucco wall. Jake clutched at his chest as he slowly slid down the wall and crumpled onto the patio floor. He couldn't get back up.

Novak rushed across the patio with a look of deadly vengeance in his eyes. He wasn't done with Jake McKenna yet. Stryker stuck out his foot and tripped the Marine. Novak went sprawling onto the stone floor. Stryker looked down at him as he said, "Okay, Novak, you've proved your point. Now let it go."

"Fuck you, Stryker. You're next, asshole!"

Stryker let the man get halfway up before he brought his huge fist up in an overhead swing that caught Novak right between the eyes and drove him back onto the floor. Novak's nose was broken. Stryker moved in for the kill.

"Stryker! That's it, goddamnit! It's over." It was the colonel. "Somebody help Mr. Novak inside. Doc, go with them. See what you can do."

"This is just fucking great! Fucking outstanding! I've got six hundred goddamn bandits and just as many NVA running around out there with this

man's daughter and three nuns who are going
through who knows what, and you people who are
supposed to be professionals are trying to tear each
other's heads off. I am embarrassed that Mr. Randolph has to stand here and watch such behavior
from the very men on whom his daughter's life
depends. There will not be another incident of this
kind. Is that understood?''

Stryker and the rest of the force were staring
down at the floor like a group of schoolkids being
scolded by their teacher.

''I said—is that understood!''

The group answered as one with a resounding
''Yes sir!''

Richards tossed the pointer he had been holding
in his hand onto a patio table. ''All right then, in
one hour we'll try to go through this one more
time. I expect every man back here and on time.''
The colonel walked past them without saying another word as he went back upstairs and to his
room. No one said anything as the group broke up,
each man going his own way. Buck and Stryker
walked along the patio with Randy York.

''Jesus, Paul, that was the last thing we needed,''
said York.

''I know Randy. But hell, Jake didn't have a lot
of options. The guy embarrassed him in front of
the whole damn group. What could he do?''

''I know that, Paul, but you guys have been riding Novak pretty hard. True, the man has a personality like a cactus, but he's got a lot of things
on his mind, too. The fact that he had four of his
boys gunned down and his boss's daughter kidnapped hasn't helped smooth out that personality.
The colonel didn't think he was much when he first

met him, either. So we did some checking. The guy has two silver stars and three bronze for valors.''

"Man! That guy did a lot of shit for an officer," said Buck.

"He wasn't an officer then, Buck. Novak earned a combat commission at the battle for the Citadel in Hue during the offensive. He was there from the beginning to the end. He lost his whole squad on the first day and formed up another one from the stragglers, leading four more assaults on the place. He was wounded three times before it was over. So you see, guys, Novak's earned his spurs.''

Stryker thought of the remarks they had been tossing at the security man. He was beginning to understand why Novak had gone off. What made it worse was the fact that Novak could be right. Jake *was* a drunk. He'd said it himself. Over the hill? Who could say? Could Jake keep it together when the shit went down? Novak had had the same questions, and was just more vocal about it. Stryker had received the same results in Sharon's kitchen. Whatever was going to happen was going to happen. It was too late to stop the operation now.

Everyone was back on time as the colonel picked up the pointer for the second time that night. Novak stood quietly by the French doors. A massive Band-Aid was across his nose. His eyes had already started to swell slightly. Jake stood on the other side of the patio. His right eye had been cleaned up, but it, too, was swollen. There was perfect silence as Richards began. "As I was saying earlier, gentlemen, at first glance, it would appear that we are going to be badly outnumbered.

However, thanks to Sergeant McKenna's years of experience in this country and his knowledge of the Meo tribe's language and their combat ability, we should have an army of our own to go against Colonel Bao or any other units we should encounter. Sergeant McKenna believes we can field an army of seven or eight hundred Meo warriors on the Plain of Jars.''

The size of the force enumerated by Richards brought low whistles from the group. The colonel continued. ''In approximately six hours, Sergeant McKenna will be parachuting into the mountains of the Xieng Khouang Province. He should be over the target area one hour before first light. Once on the ground, he will locate and link up with Muong Sing, the designated king of the Meo people. Mr. Alley has confirmed that Sing is still in charge of an area that presently contains a total of forty to fifty villages. For ten years, Sergeant McKenna has been accepted by Meo ritual as the adopted son of Chief Sing. Once the ritual has been performed it can never be broken.'' Richards paused a moment and looked at Jake as he remarked, ''Let's hope his reunion with Chief Sing will not be as zealous as his conversation with Mr. Novak.''

The remark brought a round of laughter from the men on the patio. It was a much needed respite from the earlier events. The group finally seemed more relaxed. The fight was forgotten. Richards continued. ''Sergeant McKenna is confident that he and his adopted father can organize an army which will move for the plain within thirty-six hours after his arrival. We have based the launch and movements of Lobo One and Lobo Two on that approximate time frame. Sergeant McKenna will be picked up by a C-47 Dakota in five hours. The plane will drop him over the mountains and return to this location. Twelve hours later, we will all board the aircraft and fly to Nakhon Phanom. Mr. Alley has secured us another safe house, complete with a runway and an established communications setup. The house will be Wolf Pack's base of operations. We will launch Lobos One and Two from that location.''

Richards paused, then asked, ''Gentlemen, before I proceed with the next phase of the operation, what are your questions up to this point?''

''Sir, I take it the Thai government is aware of what we are planning to do, otherwise we wouldn't be able to do all this flying back and forth across the borders. Is that correct?'' asked Stryker.

''Unofficially, yes, Paul. Mr. Randolph's contacts in the State Department and the American Embassy have reached an agreement with the Thai government. Of course, if we screw this up, they're going to swear they didn't know anything about it. More than likely a lot of folks back home will have a chance to see us on TV. Just like they did a few years ago when another SF colonel got caught using Thailand as a base site to go into Laos in search of American POWs.''

''Sir, what kind of weapons and equipment are we going to have available and when do we get them?'' asked one of the volunteers.

''Mr. Alley, would you like to handle that one?'' said Richards.

''Certainly, Erin. Gentlemen, the weapons, ammo and equipment are presently at the safe house in Nakhon Phanom. I'm afraid that due to the short notice and the importance of the time factor, we were unable to obtain some of the more high-speed weaponry. What we do have consists of M-16A2s, Car-15s, AK-50s, SAWs, Mossberg automatic 12-gauge shotguns, pump M-79 grenade launchers, and a few MP-5s. In the explosives field, we have Frags, Claymores, C-4 plastic, and a couple of cases of CS gas. Pistolwise, we've got the new 9-millimeter Berettas with the fifteen-shot clips, the Smith and Wesson 9 millimeter, the Colt .44 magnum, .357 magnum, or the Colt .45 Commander. Communications gear: the MX 300 with the whisper mikes for interteam traffic, PRC-70s, and the old reliable PRC-74s for long-distance shots. Paul, I'm sorry we couldn't convince the Thais to let us go with SATCOM, but it's kind of hard to claim you didn't know anything about a military operation going on when messages are being sent by satellite to a base in your own country.''

''No problem, Rick. If the 70s don't get through, I know the 74s can,'' said Stryker.

''That's all I've got, Erin,'' said Alley.

''Thanks, Rick. Any more questions before we continue?'' asked Richards.

There were none. Although he wasn't saying anything, Novak appeared impressed by the amount of coordination demonstrated so far. He was quietly reevaluating his opinion of Richards and his organization. A sudden throbbing pain shot along the bridge of his nose, reminding him of the possible weak link in this plan, Jake. If he was unable to hold up his end of the plan, they would all be dead meat. But what the hell, he'd already misjudged Colonel Richards. How could he be sure that he wasn't also wrong about Jake McKenna?

Richards continued with the briefing. "Men, since we don't know when Bao is scheduled to arrive in the area of the plain, it is going to be necessary for us to get in there first and establish observation points. Therefore, I have broken the group into two elements. Sergeant Stryker and Lobo One will parachute onto the plateau just north of the plain. Your drop time will be midnight tomorrow night. Sergeant Buchanan and Lobo Two will be dropped in at oh-one-hundred hours on the plateau to the west. If you will look at the charts, you'll find your name and which element you have been assigned to for the remainder of this operation. Mr. Novak, I assume you have jumped from an airplane before."

Novak stared at the chart. He was assigned to Buchanan's element. Hell, he'd forgotten that these SF types never walked anywhere if they could throw themselves out of an airplane instead. He'd done a lot of things in his life, but throwing himself out of a perfectly good airplane wasn't one of them.

"No . . . no, Colonel. I'm . . . I'm afraid not."

Randolph looked over at Burford and smiled. Richards had caught it too. Although he never changed expressions, Richards had a feeling that it was all coming together. Novak had addressed him as Colonel.

Richards nodded toward Stryker. "Paul, you take care of that when we get upcountry."

"Roger, sir."

Randy York couldn't help but smile as he saw the look on Novak's face. He was willing to bet the Marine would rather take on another Tet offensive than make a night drop into Laos.

"Jake, you will attempt to make contact with

Lobos One and Two every hour on the hour beginning at oh-three-hundred hours. Both elements should be off the DZs and into an R.O.N. site by that time. Once communications are established between all three elements, Lobo One will notify Wolf Pack that commo linkup has been established. Lobo One and Two, at first light you will select a good observation point and move into position. Lobo, you will notify us when you and your element are ready to move down from the mountains. One and Two, you will monitor, but not transmit, unless an emergency arises. The less traffic we have coming out of there, the better off we're going to be.''

Stryker and Buchanan both nodded in agreement.

''Okay, boys, here comes the part I'm sure you've all been waiting for—how you're getting out of there once the party's over. Again we owe Mr. Alley a debt of thanks—and of course, Mr. Randolph and his checkbook.''

There were a few amens mixed with laughter.

''We have been able to borrow three UH1H helicopters from an agency that shall remain anonymous. However, they could not provide the necessary pilots, mainly because they're not supposed to know this is going on. Fortunately, there are still a number of chopper pilots left over from the Vietnam era living in Bangkok. They are more than willing to earn a bag full of money for doing a little flying. The choppers and pilots will be in Nakhon Phanom tomorrow afternoon. Once we have all our elements in position and a confirmation that Bao has the women, the operation will be in the hands of Sergeant Stryker. Paul, you're going to have to call it from there on out. Once we have the women, all elements will move to the eastern end of the plain and provide cover fire for the choppers. Of course, the women and wounded will go out on the first lift. Stryker controls the extractions. Well, there you have it, men. I know it's not the best plan you've ever heard, but it's all we have. You're all the best in the business. I know you want this to work as bad as I do. Not only for Mr. Randolph and his daughter but also for a chance to show the Communists what we could have done in Vietnam without the politicians. Now, if there are no more questions, I suggest that those who are not involved in the operation going on later tonight get some sleep while they can. That's all, gentlemen.''

Randolph came over and shook the colonel's hand as he said, ''My God, Colonel, I had no idea what was involved in this. I want you to know, I don't think I could have found a better man to handle it. I believe you even impressed Mr. Novak. Thank you.''

''No. Thank you, sir. The planning is the easy part.'' Nodding in the direction of his troops as they were going inside, he said, ''They're the ones who have to make it work. A lot of them are not going to make it back, and they know it. However, they wouldn't miss it for the world. God help us if there ever comes a day we can't find men like these.''

Burford asked, ''Colonel, weren't you going to have the men fill out wills and insurance policies tonight?''

''I haven't forgotten, Mr. Burford. I just felt they

had enough to think about tonight. We'll do it to-morrow.''

''Of course. Also, what about the gold in the bank?''

''Already spent, Mr. Burford.''

Richards watched the little man turn slightly pale as he asked, ''My God! You mean all . . . all that gold is already gone?''

''Yes, sir. Government cooperation and weapons are high this year, along with the cost of airplanes, helicopters and houses with runways in the back yard. You see, Mr. Burford, everything in this life costs money, everything. With the dollar bouncing up and down, gold is the only answer.''

Randolph nodded in agreement as he placed his arm around his vice president and said, ''And fortunately, Edward, I have all the money that any one man could ever want in this lifetime, and if it takes every last nickel I've got to get my daughter back, then so be it.''

''Of course, sir, I understand that. I just never realized how complicated something like this really was. Colonel, I must say, for a man like myself, who knows very little about military tactics or planning, I find your briefing very thought-provoking and highly professional. I compliment you, sir.''

''Thank you, Mr. Burford. Now if you gentlemen will pardon me. There are a few minor details that Major York and I must work out before the plane arrives. Excuse me.''

The businessmen watched Richards as he left the patio and disappeared into the darkness. Randolph said, ''Quite an impressive man, isn't he, Edward?''

"Yes sir. I must admit I had many doubts about this when we started. However, if there's any chance of getting Denise back, I firmly believe these are the men who can do it."

"God, I hope you're right, Edward. Come on. I'll buy you a drink."

Randolph allowed Burford to go through the French doors first as he paused. Looking back into the darkness, he said a silent prayer.

Chapter 11

The crew chief reached down to unlatch the cargo door. A rush of warm air moved through the aircraft as the door was thrown open. Below, in the darkness, lay the mountains of Laos. Turning to the sole passenger in the plane, the chief yelled, "Ten minutes!"

Jake McKenna waved as he acknowledged the amount of time he had left before reaching the release point. He had only ten minutes to reconsider an entire lifetime, both the good and the bad.

Everyone had been at the airstrip to wish him luck, even Novak. Nevertheless, it was Paul Stryker's words that now ran through his mind. Hugging him unashamedly, Paul had whispered, "Get it done, Jake, and watch your ass. When this is over, we're gonna work on that other problem you have—you, me, Sharon, and Charlotte. You can count on it."

Jake had found hope in Paul's words. Together, and with Charlotte's help, he knew there was still a chance. A chance for him to be the loving husband and father he had once been.

"Six minutes!"

God, he wished he could have held her in his arms one more time before he left. He needed to tell her he knew he had been wrong and that he loved her so very much. He longed to hear the words "Dad, I love you" from the son who had grown into a fine young man despite an absentee military father. He ached to hug his daughter and hear her say, as she always had when he had left, "Daddy, we love you." Her eyes always filled with tears as she spoke the words. There had been a lot of good-byes over the years, too many. Damnit, he would work this thing out! Too many people cared about him to let everything slip away so easily.

"One minute!"

Jake McKenna rose to his feet and casually hooked his static line to the anchor cable as he had done countless times over the last twenty-odd years. Standing in the door with the warm night winds blowing around him, he felt so alone. Memories of a song he'd heard once on the TV show "Miami Vice" flashed through his mind. It was something about the air and the night calling him. Looking down into the darkness, he saw Charlotte's face; tears were in her eyes.

"Go! Go!" screamed the crew chief as the red light on the side of the door flicked to green.

Jake McKenna threw himself out of the plane and into the blackness of the night. A loud pop echoed through the aircraft, followed by a banging, rattling sound that reverberated its way into the cockpit.

The co-pilot yelled into his mike, "Christ, Chief, what the hell was that?"

"My God! The anchor cable broke!" came the chief's frantic reply.

"Did his chute open?"

"I don't know! I don't know! It's darker than hell out there!"

"Can you bring in the cable?"

"I'll try," said the chief. The pilot could hear the heavy breathing as the man worked.

"Oh, God, please, please."

The C-47 banked hard. Both pilots strained their eyes for any sign of an open parachute. There was nothing there. They couldn't stay in the area, they had to get back across the border. The pilots waited for word from the crew chief. The co-pilot finally asked, "Chief, what did you get?"

There was a long pause, then, "Nothing, sir. The anchor cable's clean."

The two pilots looked at each other wondering if the chute had deployed before the cable broke or even as it was coming apart. If the snap hook had caught on the U-bolt attached to the end of the cable, it would have opened Jake's chute, leaving the deployment bag hung on the end, but there was no D-bag on the cable that the chief had pulled into the aircraft. Jake McKenna was gone. . . .

"Damnit," said Buck as he slammed his big fist down on the table next to the radios and walked away.

Burford felt like he was going to be sick as he thought of McKenna falling to his death from that height. Randolph stood next to Richards as the colonel spoke into the mike once more, "Midnight Rider, this is Wolf Pack. Confirm. There was no chute. Is that a roger? Over."

"Roger that, Wolf Pack. We saw no canopy. The U-bolt was still attached to the end of the cable, and we have no D-bag. Say again, no D-bag. Over.''

Novak walked over to the window where Stryker stood staring out into the night. ''Sergeant Stryker, I'm . . . I'm sorry about Jake.''

Stryker turned and looked at the man. He knew Novak's words were sincere. ''Jake wouldn't have wanted it any other way. Thank you, Mr. Novak.''

''The name's Derek.''

Erin Richards felt as if a part of him had died with Jake. Wiping the tears from his eyes, he walked outside. Randolph followed him. Both men stood silently watching the pre-gray dawn make its way along the horizon. They both knew a decision had to be made, and it had to be made now. Without Jake and his army of Meo, they knew the mission would be sheer suicide.

''It's over, isn't it, Erin?'' Randolph's words were painful.

''Yes, Johnathan, I'm afraid it is. What little chance we had is now gone.''

Even though Randolph knew what the answer was going to be, when it came, it tore the heart right out of him. Jake was gone; and now, so was his little girl. He wanted to say something, but he had no words. Randolph walked away with tears running down his cheeks. His thoughts turned to the memory of a little blond girl with sparkling blue eyes running into his arms.

Stryker, Buck, and Novak came out of the radio shack and stood by Richards.

''We figure the plane should land in about thirty minutes, Colonel. One hour for refit and refuel and we should be ready to lift off again by oh-eight-hundred for Nakhon Phanom,'' said Stryker.

Richards turned to the three men with a sense of pride; they hadn't given up hope. Nonetheless, the reality of the situation overshadowed the bravery of these men. "No, Paul, it's over. We lost before we started. There's nothing that we can do now. Jake was the key. Now, he's gone. That's enough."

"Well, sir, you and Randy can head on back if you want, but we're still going in after those women. We've already talked it over with the boys and they've all agreed. We're still going for it," said Stryker.

Richards stared at them in wonder. They had made up their minds. He could see it in their eyes. They were determined to see this thing through to the end.

"My God, Paul, you and Buck know this is suicide. Hell, Novak, you didn't even believe it would work when we had Jake. I don't hear you saying anything now. Talk some sense into these two, will you?"

"Can't do that, Colonel. The history books are full of the names of people who never had a chance, but they went for it anyway. Hell, we're already here so we might as well give it a shot," said Novak with a smile.

"Amen, brother," said Buck.

"Like you said, sir, it's already cost us. We owe it to Jake and those women to at least try," said Stryker.

Randolph came up to the group just as Richards asked, "Are you all sure you want to do this?"

"All the way, sir," said Stryker.

"What's going on, Colonel?" asked Randolph.

"We're going after your daughter, Johnathan."

"But that's . . . that's not possible. It's . . ."

"Don't waste your time, Johnathan, they've already made up their minds. It's a go. We have a lot to do before we move out of here. Buck, you go break the news to Rick Alley. After he comes out of shock, tell him I want an intell update from some of his old friends in the capital. Stryker, you and Novak get the rest of the people ready. Let's move it, people. You're not getting paid by the hour."

Randolph watched in amazement as the three saluted and left. Burford came up to Randolph and asked, "When are we going home, sir?"

"We're not, Edward, not without Denise. You know, they say there are no more heroes. Well, they're wrong, Edward. Thank God, they're so wrong."

Randolph and Richards went into the house, leaving a bewildered Burford to ponder Randolph's words. . . .

Chapter 12

Colonel Kloskov halted the convoy at an isolated guard post along Highway 13. Major Thieu remained with the trucks and the gold. Colonel Diem and Kloskov drove to the village of Ban Namay for a meeting with the commanders of the three NVA companies which Diem had requested.

The three young captains saluted smartly as the two colonels stepped from their jeep. Diem introduced them to Colonel Kloskov, then asked, "Where are your troops?"

Captain Lin Song stepped forward. As the oldest, he would serve as the spokesman for the group. "They are hidden in the valley along the western edge of the plain, sir."

"Very good. It is imperative that they not be seen until we are ready. Have any of you been briefed on your mission here?"

"No, sir. We were informed that we would receive our instructions once you arrived."

Removing a map from the jeep, Diem called the officers around him as he spread the map on the hood of the vehicle.

"In less than thirty-six hours, the bandit leader, Bao, and his army of thugs will meet with Colonel Kloskov and myself on the Plain of Jars. He expects to trade four American women that he kidnapped for weapons, ammunition, and a large sum of gold. It is our intention to make it appear as if we are going through with his demands. When in fact, we intend to eliminate the outlaw and his entire band of parasites. This is a directive from our commanders in Hanoi. Our Russian friends have concurred with this decision as well.''

Kloskov observed that the mission seemed to meet with approval from all three of the young Vietnamese officers. Bao had few friends, if any, among the North Vietnamese. To them, he was a ruthless man who had used the war to gratify his need for killing, raping, and plundering the countryside, using the Vietnamese cause as justification for his actions.

Colonel Diem continued. ''It is vitally important that the women are exchanged and secure before any shooting begins. I cannot stress the importance of this enough, Comrades. They must not be placed at any risk. Do you understand?''

The three captains nodded as Song asked, ''How will we know when to attack, Comrade Colonel?''

Kloskov walked to the rear of the jeep. Pulling the long radio antenna that was affixed to the side of the vehicle downward, he tied a white rag around the top and released the antenna. It sprang upward, making the white cloth easily visible. Colonel Diem said, ''We shall have that cloth tied in that position when we go to make the exchange. Bao will think of it only as a signal of truce. Once Major Thieu has the women, and they are a safe distance away, Colonel Kloskov will step to the rear of the jeep and pull the antenna down as if to remove the cloth. That will be your signal to begin your attack on the bandits."

The NVA officers appeared apprehensive. Kloskov concluded, "Captain Song, you and your fellow officers appear worried. Is there a problem?"

"Yes, Comrade Colonel. When we open fire, you and Colonel Diem will be in the midst of the bandits. Bao will realize you have tricked him and will bring the full force of his men against the two of you."

"That is not important, Captain Song. Colonel Kloskov and I have already discussed that possibility. The safety of the women and the elimination of Bao and his cursed army is all that matters. Hopefully, one of us will manage to kill Bao when the battle begins."

Kloskov said, "We ask only that, should we both be killed, you and your men wipe out Bao's army to the last man. Therefore our death would not have been in vain."

"It shall be done, Comrade. You have our word," said Song with a sense of pride at having the opportunity to know two such brave men.

Removing three pieces of paper from his shirt pocket, Diem passed them out to the captains. "These are the radio frequencies we will use for this operation. You will monitor your radios beginning at dawn tomorrow. I will give you your final orders on when to disburse your men once we know Bao's approach route. Are there any questions?"

"No sir," said Song.

"Good," replied Diem as he saluted. "Until tomorrow."

The officers returned the salute. With pride, they looked upon the face of this old warrior who thought nothing of standing in the middle of a pack of wolves and giving up his life. They held their salutes as a sign of honor until both officers had driven away. Walking out of the village, one of the officers said, "If Buddha is smiling on Colonel Diem tomorrow, he might survive."

"I fear even a smile from the great Buddha will not be enough, my friend. That was what the colonel was telling us. He and Kloskov are dead men . . . and they know it."

It was four in the afternoon when Colonel Richards and his force arrived at Nakhon Phanom. Weapons, ammo, and equipment were issued. The men busied themselves cleaning their weapons, loading magazines, and rigging their rucksacks and web gear. Canteens were filled, straps taped down, and fingers were cut out of black leather gloves. Strobe lights, first aid packs and knives were taped to the shoulder straps of the web gear for quick access. The rucks were small, but well constructed of a new lightweight alloy. They had considered going in without the rucksacks. After all, if everything went as planned, Lobos One and Two would be in and out in twenty-four hours. Stryker had vetoed the idea. If things didn't go right, the survivors would need supplies to sustain them while trying to E&E back into Thailand.

Burford and Randolph stood silently in the doorway of the team house watching the men go about their preparations for battle. Burford remarked, "It's just like a business, isn't it, Johnathan?"

"Yes, Edward. A dangerous and deadly business."

The sound of approaching helicopters diverted

their attention from the team. Walking out into the courtyard, they watched as a formation of three UH1H choppers circled the house and began their descent on the far side of the runway across from the C-47. Colonel Richards and Randy York came out of the house. Richards asked the two men if they would like to take a closer look at the helicopters and meet the pilots.

"Certainly, Colonel," answered Randolph.

"You might as well come along, Mr. Burford. It'll give you a chance to see where a large chunk of your gold went."

"Thank you, Colonel. I believe I will."

Each chopper carried three men: a pilot, a copilot, and a crew chief who also served as a door gunner. Richards waited until the pilots had gone to complete shutdown and the rotors had stopped turning before he approached the aircraft.

Neither Randolph nor Burford was prepared for the sight that emerged from the helicopters. Stryker and his men at least looked and acted military, but these people, the crews, wore a mismatch of civilian and military clothing. They wore fatigue shirts with all types of military insignia and a variety of sergeant's stripes, some sewn on upside down, and blue jeans, cowboy boots, and cowboy hats. Some wore fatigue pants with brightly colored Hawaiian shirts. There was a variety of baseball hats, football jerseys, long hair, short hair, no hair, beards, and handlebar mustaches. One big man had a patch over one eye. Some had shoulder holsters with automatic pistols. The cowboys wore western-style holsters and carried six-shooters. They looked more like gunfighters than pilots.

Randolph took particular interest in the weapon

the one-eyed man had hanging from his belt by a snap link. It was a sawed-off M-79 grenade launcher. The stock had been cut down and formed into a pistol grip. A U-bolt was attached at the end of the short barrel. The weapon was no longer than twelve inches. The bolt kept the end of the barrel from splitting out when it was fired.

Richards and York both laughed as the colonel said, "Don't worry, gentlemen, they may not look it, but these are some of the hottest chopper jockeys to come out of the Southeast Asian War. They cost you plenty, Mr. Randolph—but they're going to be worth every penny before this is over."

One-Eye led the crews as they walked up to Richards. Burford took a step back. They were a rough-looking bunch of men.

"Erin! Randy! You're both lookin' damn good for a couple of old retired fucks," said One-Eye.

Richards grinned as he replied, "That's because you're only looking out of one eye, you old bastard."

"Yeah," said York. "Is that a beer gut hanging out there or did some little Thai girl knock you up?"

Everyone was laughing.

"Mr. Randolph, Mr. Burford, I'd like you to meet Mitch Bacher, the best damn chopper pilot to come out of Vietnam. Mitch, these are your employers."

Bacher stepped forward and extended his big hand. The leather-tough face smiled and there was a twinkle in his one blue-gray eye as he said, "Nice to meet you fellows." He gave each man a firm Texas-style handshake. He then turned to the others and said, "Well get on up here, you bunch of degenerates, and shake hands with the folks that're payin' the bills for this little shindig.''

Bacher ran through the introductions as the men filed past. Theirs were names that Burford knew he'd never forget—Bud ''Tit-man'' Tillman, Kevin ''Big Mo'' Morano, Steven ''The Man'' Graham, Brian ''Hard Case'' Hartman, and Dave ''Go Low'' Rowe.

Burford thought he was seeing double as Bacher introduced the Shanassey brothers. ''Guess you already noticed that these boys are twins. The one with the long hair is Mark. We call him 'The Snake.' And this is Donny. Don't pay any attention to that earring hangin' off his ear. The boy's a real badass.''

The last man to come forward sent a chill through Burford. He was the biggest man he'd ever seen, standing at least six-foot-six, and was built like a house with wide shoulders and bulging muscles that strained against the confines of the L.A. Raiders T-shirt he wore. The man's chest looked like a piece of granite. He wore an olive-drab rag tied around his head. His hair was short and he was clean shaven. As Burford shook hands with the giant, he stared into the man's dark brown eyes. There was nothing there: no acknowledgement, no reaction, nothing. They were cold, desolate eyes that lived in a world of their own.

Bacher said, ''Fellows, this is J. J. Johnson. You won't find a better man with a machine gun on a chopper or on the ground. Handles the damn thing like it was a natural part of his body.''

Rick Alley, Stryker, and Buck came out on the front steps of the house. Buck yelled, ''Hey, you bunch of over-the-hill fucks want something to eat?''

Bacher and his crew recognized the three men on the steps. Their laughter was mixed with a number of insults as they moved to the front of the house.

Richards turned to York and Burford. ''Randy, will you and Mr. Burford see that the quarters are ready for our new arrivals?''

''Sure thing, Erin.''

Stryker strolled up to Bacher and the colonel. Sticking his hand out, he said, ''Mitch, damn glad to see Rick hired the best.''

''How you doin', Paul?''

''Takin' it a day at a time, Mitch.''

Sadly, Bacher said, ''Rick got word to us about Jake. Are you sure he didn't make it?''

''It's a good bet he didn't, Mitch. We checked the aircraft when it landed. There was blood on the right tail section and some structure damage. Something hit it pretty hard,'' said Stryker, looking down at the ground.

''Jesus, Paul, I'm sorry to hear that. If it hadn't been for Jake neither one of us would be standing here right now.''

Mitch Bacher had flown the chopper carrying Stryker and his team the day they were shot down in Vietnam. Jake had pulled Bacher from the burning chopper minutes before it had exploded. McKenna had received his CMH and Bacher had lost an eye.

The mention of Jake cast a solemn silence over the men. Buck called to them from the front porch, ''You boys wanta eat, you better get in here. Bacher ain't fed these animals for a week, and they're eatin' everything but the damn floor.''

The remark brought smiles from the group and it seemed to break the gloom that had momentarily come over them.

''Mitch, we'll get some chow, then we'll brief you and the boys on the operation. It's going to be a tough one,'' said Colonel Richards.

''Hell, Colonel, for the kind of money Mr. Randolph here is putting out, we'd take on Rambo and the whole fuckin' Russian army.''

Johnathan Randolph was beginning to understand these men, their sense of undying loyalty, and their need for adventure and living on the edge. Humor was used to conceal the fear they did not want to admit to. Randolph could understand that. He was doing the same thing. Walking back to the house he smiled as he said, ''Mr. Bacher, the Russian army, maybe. But Rambo—you might want to reconsider that one.''

The men were in a jubilant mood as they went up the steps and into the house. Across the airstrip, the crew chief was refueling the C-47. It was five in the afternoon. In seven hours they would be flying over the Laotian mountains once again, and at midnight a small group of men would cast their fate to the winds. . . .

The day's march had been extremely hard on the women. The rugged hills and the thick jungle had even begun to take their toll on Bao's troops. Phong had tried to ease the hardship on the women by calling for continuous breaks along the route; this began to irritate Bao. He wanted to be at the base of the plain by sundown. Now, with only an hour left before nightfall, he was still two miles from his objective. Moving back along the line, he kicked and slapped at his men, cussing at them to get to their feet and keep moving. Denise was pouring water onto a rag and gently rubbing it over Sister Helen's face. The heat and her age had driven her to the verge of exhaustion. Bao's voice proclaimed his irritation. "Get that old woman on her feet, goddamnit. We are moving again, and we will not stop until we are at the plain." Turning to Phong, he yelled, "Do you understand, Captain?"

Maria saw the look of hatred fill Phong's eyes as he stared hard at the bandit leader. The look did not go unnoticed by Bao.

"Surely you are not contemplating an act of ignorance, are you, Captain? I realize you have developed a feeling of affection for these American sluts, but they are not worth dying for. However, I find your concern very touching."

Bao's open hand caught Phong unprepared as the solid sound of his slap drew the attention of everyone around them. "Now get these bitches on their feet before I blow your fucking head off."

Bao had drawn his gun after the slap and now had it pointed at Phong. The barrel was less than two inches from the captain's face. Maria yelled, "No! Please. We'll move. See—we'll get Sister Helen up. Please don't shoot!"

A small trickle of blood made its way down the captain's chin. Bao stepped back. Glancing at Maria, he considered killing Phong simply because she had asked him not to. The only thing stopping him was the look of anxiety on the faces of some of his men. Phong was well liked by many of them. Lowering his gun, he said, "Do not tempt me again, Captain. Now move! We have wasted enough time.''

The troops began to file past. No one looked at the captain. Maria took the rag from Denise and wiped the blood from Phong's chin.

''Thank you, Sister.'' Her touch erased the hatred from his eyes. Maria smiled, then helped Denise and Monica with Sister Helen. Phong fell in behind them as they made their way up the winding trail. Touching the corner of his split lip, Phong swore he would kill Bao before this affair was over. . . .

Stryker completed his jump master checks on Novak's equipment. The ex-Marine had reevaluated his opinion of Richards and his assault force. They were every bit the professionals the colonel had claimed they were. Even the wild-looking chopper crews had impressed him during the briefing on the extraction plan. If they could get the women away from the bandits, he knew the chopper boys, code-named Eagle's Wing, would get them out.

''Okay, Novak. You're go to go. How you feelin'?'' asked Stryker.

''Scared shitless,'' came the nervous reply.

''That's great. Keep that attitude, and you'll be fine,'' laughed Buck.

Richards, Randolph, York, and Burford were standing off the runway watching the preparations. Alley came over to them.

''Erin, I just got confirmation from my boys across the border. The NVA have moved three companies of regulars to a village just beyond the plain. A convoy was spotted just off Highway Thirteen. They're heading for the same area. They also found two of Bao's men hanging from a tree in an abandoned campsite. Bao's definitely headed for the Plain of Jars.''

''Jake had it pegged right,'' said Richards. ''They're having the meet on the plain to make the exchange. Randy, you and Rick let Stryker know about this. Mr. Randolph and I are going to the operations and communications room. You both join us there after takeoff.''

''Roger, sir,'' said York as he turned to head for the C-47. Rick Alley didn't move. Staring down at the ground, he quietly said, ''Erin, there's one more thing. My men located part of a parachute hanging in the trees. There . . . there was a body up there, too.''

''Did they try to get it down?''

''No, it was pretty high up, and they thought they heard people coming, so they left it and took off. I thought you should know.''

''Yes . . . thanks Rick. When you see Stryker, let him know. Guess we were all hoping for an outside chance that Jake made it. That kind of closes the books, I suppose.''

Alley nodded as he and York headed for the team house. Rick's news had once again cast a spell of gloom over the mission.

''Erin, I am truly sorry,'' said Randolph.

''I am, too, Johnathan. What's done is done. Nothing can change it.''

No more was said as the three men walked silently to the operations room. As they entered, Burford felt a slight fluttering in the pit of his stomach as he whispered, ''It's started. My God, they're going to do it.''

Mitch Bacher had opted to fly with the team. Serving as the safety, he would help the crew chief retrieve the static lines after the team exited the aircraft. Stryker, like Richards, had refused to accept the fact that Jake was dead. Alley's news had squashed any hope he had held for Jake.

During the pilots' briefing, the matter of two separate drop times had been discussed in detail. It was finally decided that both teams would be put out on the same lift. Lobo One with Stryker, Doc, and eight of Richards's men sat on the right side. Lobo Two with Buck, Merrill, and Novak sat on the left. Mitch yelled back from the cockpit, "Paul, we're ready if you are."

"Well, fuck it. Let's go party!"

The C-47 taxied to the far end of the strip, swung its tail around, and revved its twin engines to max RPMs. Mitch released the brake and the big bird lumbered down the runway gaining speed. The wheels lifted off the ground just as they passed York and Alley, who were standing off to the side of the hardtop. Both men waved as the plane lifted into the warm night air and disappeared into the darkness.

"Now comes the hard part," said York.

"Yeah," said Alley, "the waiting."

The sound of the engines faded as the two men walked back into the house. . . .

In the soft glow of the red light that bathed the aircraft's interior, Stryker studied the faces of the men who were about to jump into hell with him. Bobby Joe Baker leaned his head on crossed arms that rested on his reserve; he was already asleep. Doc seemed to be staring off into the far reaches of his mind, perhaps thinking of Angola and Namba. Merrill and Buck were laughing about something. Stryker couldn't hazard a guess as to what they were laughing about, but it didn't really matter; different people handled fear in different ways. Novak shifted nervously in his seat, trying to find a comfortable position, something that even experienced paratroops had found impossible. The weight of the main chute, the reserve in the front, the steel pot that constantly gave you headaches, and worst of all, the rucksack that hung in the front, rubbing against your knees, did not add up to comfort. Also the weapon that was strapped to all of this equipment precluded any relief on the left side. Novak suddenly remembered why he'd never cared to go to airborne school: it was uncomfortable as hell.

The other members of the team were all from Richards's security firm. He was right; they were all young. Stryker would have preferred to have some of the boys from the old days with him, but there hadn't been time for extended recruitment. Leaning back, he lit a cigarette and thought of Jake and how ironic it was for him to have died that way. Jake had completed over a thousand jumps and survived countless firefights, only to be killed by a defective piece of cable. When he got back— if he got back—he would explain what had happened to Sharon. Together, they would take the money from Jake's insurance to Charlotte and the kids. He would have to take Sharon; he couldn't face Charlotte alone.

Bacher came down from the cockpit and yelled to Stryker, "Ten minutes, Paul!"

Stryker struggled to his feet. Moving to the cen-

ter of the plane and facing the team, he raised both
hands as he pushed his arms outward, palms up,
and yelled, "Ten minutes!"

Someone woke up Bobby Joe as the others began shifting in their seats. Novak felt his stomach
tighten. A cold sweat formed along his forehead.
The crew chief leaned forward and said something
to Stryker. Stryker nodded, then turned back to the
team. Raising his hands again, he spread one hand
forward and uplifted a finger on the other, "Six
minutes!"

The crew chief threw the door open. A rush of
warm air raced through the plane. Novak's hands
were sweating.

"Get ready!" yelled Stryker, as he began the
jump commands.

"Outboard personnel, stand up!"

Lobo One fought to steady themselves as they
gained their footing and stood.

"Inboard personnel, stand up!"

"Hook up!"

Novak's hands were shaking as he tried to snap
the hook of his static line to the anchor cable.
Bacher, seeing the problem, made his way down
the aisle. Taking the hook from Novak, he snapped
the line to the cable and smiled at the Marine.
Slapping Novak on the butt, he gave him a thumbs-
up.

"Check static lines!"

"Sound off for equipment check!"

Twenty, okay; nineteen, okay; eighteen, okay—
the count worked its way up to Buck.

Feeling the man behind him slap him on the ass,
Buck yelled, "All okay!"

Pointing to Buchanan, then the door, Stryker yelled, "Stand in the door!"

Buck stepped forward and positioned himself in the doorway of the C-47. The team closed up behind him. Stryker kept his eyes on the red glow of the ready lights. Suddenly they flicked and went green.

"Go!" screamed Stryker.

Buck pulled against the outer edges of the doorway as he threw himself out of the plane. The rest of Lobo Two followed him in rapid succession. Even Novak was caught up in the excitement, yelling "Oh shit!" as he pushed past Stryker and disappeared out the door. The C-47 banked and headed left. The red light was back on now. In five minutes the plane was back on the track and making its second approach.

"One minute!" yelled Stryker as he pointed to Doc, then the doorway again. "Stand in the door!"

Doc Shannon moved into position. The red light went green.

"Go! Go! Go!"

Shannon was up and out in less than a second, followed by Lobo One. Stryker waited until the last man went out, then smiled at Bacher. "Don't be late for the party, Mitch."

Stryker dove out the door and into the night. The chief and Bacher recovered the deployment bags and static lines as the C-47 headed back for Thailand.

Colonel Kloskov finished his coffee and lit a cigarette. Major Thieu offered him another cup, but the Russian waved it off. Colonel Diem accepted. The chest of gold sat across from them in the corner. The major moved about the tent with an exceptional amount of lively energy. Caffeine and anticipation of the forthcoming action had the young officer keyed up to the point that sleep was impossible. The two older officers sat silently thinking of the soon-to-be-fought battle, but in a different light. Diem had no illusions about what the morning would bring—fighting and death, and this time he would be one of those who would lie among the dead. It was something he had expected all his life. A life that had known little peace; there had been the French, the Japanese, the Americans, and now an army of Laotians. He had fought against them all, and each time he thought he had achieved victory there came another aggressor. Sipping his coffee, he found a strange comfort in knowing that, if nothing else, the morning would bring him final peace.

Kloskov, on the other hand, had no great desire to die. However, it was a professional hazard that he had accepted a long time ago. The military was his life. In the early years of the Vietnam War against the Americans, he had been an advisor in Hanoi. Often, he had ventured from the safety of the city and into the jungles to test the combat ability of the Americans. He rated them equal in determination, but seriously lacking in political understanding of the reasons for which they fought. Although he had some close and near-fatal encounters with the Americans during that war, nothing could compare to the suffering and bitterness he had endured in Afghanistan. He had spent three long and torturous years in that mountainous country. Wounded three times, he had quickly developed a warrior's respect for the ragged-looking men of the mountains. They dared to wage a war against modern technology with only ancient tactics and worn-out rifles. Even though Laos was not the Garden of Eden, and knowing what the morning might bring, he would still rather be here than back in those godforsaken mountains of Afghanistan.

Colonel Diem set his empty coffee cup in the center of the table and stood up. "It is late, my friends, and we have much to do tomorrow. I would suggest a few hours' sleep."

"I agree," said Kloskov, as he rose and moved to the entrance of the tent.

Major Thieu stood to follow the Russian outside. It was a cool night and the stars filled the sky. "I will see you in the morning, Colonel."

"Major Thieu, you have a family, don't you?"

"Why . . . yes, sir."

"When did you see them last?"

"Three months ago, sir."

Kloskov stared up at the stars as his voice became a near whisper. "Three months . . . I have not seen my wife or child for over two years now. My daughter Nathasia's birthday is only a week away. I miss them, Major."

"Perhaps after this business with Bao is over you can go home, Comrade Colonel."

"No, Major. Tomorrow will be my last—" Kloskov suddenly stopped talking. In the far distance a falling star streaked its way across the heavens. "You had better go to bed, Major. Tomorrow will be a busy day for all of us."

At 0300 hours, Lobo One made contact with Richards. The team was together and had suffered only minor injuries on the jump. They had not made contact with Lobo Two, but were still trying. York plotted the team's location on the map as Rick brought in another pot of coffee. No one would be getting any sleep until this thing was over.

At 0330 hours, Buck came up on the radio. Lobo Two had regrouped and was moving for an R.O.N. site. There were no injuries, and Novak was doing fine; however, he had expressed no desire to repeat the experience. Contact was made with Stryker. All elements were now in contact. The teams would move at first light for the Plain of Jars.

Chapter 13

Dawn broke as Bao sent out the first of three patrols that would monitor any movement across or around the plain. He and the main party would arrive at that location no later than 0830 hours. The squad leaders were to report immediately any movement or large gathering of troops that they might find either on the plain or while en route.

Major Thieu woke the truck drivers. Colonels Diem and Kloskov loaded the gold into their jeep and checked their weapons. The sound of the big two-and-a-half-ton trucks starting their engines thundered through the jungle.

Stryker broke Lobo One down further into two five-man teams. He had one element and Doc had the other moving 200 yards on his left. They worked out a pattern of signals that could be sent by simply pressing the squelch switch on their MX 300 radios. One press—moving. Two—halting the squad. Three times—we have movement or visual contact with the bad guys. So far they had only had to send signals that they were moving or stopping. The slopes that led up to the west side of the plain were already in sight.

Buck and Novak had taken the point for their team. Merrill was watching the back door. Before them lay the eastern slopes of the plain. They had not seen or heard anything during their move. Nevertheless, a sixth sense that comes only from years of training and combat experience told Buchanan that something was wrong.

Doc halted his element while he checked the map. The Laotian voices that he heard to his immediate right were not loud, but clear and distinct. They were close and moving right at him. The other four members of his squad had already gone to ground as he pressed the radio switch three times rapidly. Then he went flat on the ground himself.

Stryker stopped his team and waved for them to go down. The adrenaline was pumping wildly through Novak's body as he gripped the handle of his rifle. It had been a lot of years since he had played this game. Nothing had changed, he was still scared. Stryker had started to call Shannon and tell him to use the knives if they had to take anyone out, but it was too late for that now. He couldn't risk someone hearing the call. He would just have to wait and hope for the best.

Doc raised his head slightly, parting the grass in front of him carefully with his fingers. He saw them. There were seven of them. Judging from their dress, they were bandits. If they kept moving in the same direction, they were going to walk right over the team. He looked to the man next him as he reached up to the left strap of his LBE. Quietly, he pulled the knife from its scabbard and signaled for the others to do the same. Once they were ready, Doc put his finger to his lips and slowly brought another finger across his throat. No words were necessary. There was one thing in the team's favor: the seven bandits were grouped closely together. The lead man brought them to the very edge of the area where the team was hiding. The leader paused and pointed to the slopes, saying something in Laotian Doc couldn't understand. Shannon knew he had to get them to turn away from the team. Their chances were better if they could jump them from behind. A kid named Brian Jones lying next to Doc must have read the man's mind. Slowly moving his hand, Jones picked up a small rock to toss over the seven and into the brush, hoping that the sound would distract the bandits. Doc nodded for him to go ahead. Everyone silently laid their rifles aside and dug in their push-off foot. They would all go at the same time. Jones threw the rock. It hit in the dry brush beyond and behind the Laotians. Shannon's only thought as he leaped forward was that they had to take them down without a shot being fired.

Shannon body blocked two of the men. Jones took out two more with a block worthy of the L.A. Raiders. The other three members of the team leaped on the remaining three and going one-on-one made quick work of the surprised bandits. Jones swung his knife in a savage stroke to open one man's throat as clean as a surgeon. Doc slammed his blade into one man's back as he kicked out with his right foot and sent the other bandit backwards to the ground, where two members of the team fell on him, burying their blades to the hilt in his chest. Jones brought his elbow up quick, catching his second man square on the nose. As the man grabbed his shattered nose, Jones clamped his hand over the man's mouth and, jerking the head back, cut the bandit's throat. It was all over in less than a minute.

Dragging the bodies into the dense jungle brush, the men picked up their weapons and waited while Doc made contact with Stryker on the radio.

"One Alpha. One Bravo, over."

"Go Doc," came the reply.

"We had some visitors. Got seven down hard—all bandits. We must be in the right ballpark. Over."

"Roger, Doc. Let's give it another two hundred yards forward and go for linkup. More than likely those boys were the advance party. There's bound to be more of them around here somewhere. Watch your ass, doc. One Alpha, out."

Shannon slapped Jones on the back and grinned. Any doubts he had about Richards's people had disappeared. They quietly moved out. Two hundred more yards would put them at the base of the slope.

Buck had monitored the radio conversation. He told Novak and Merrill about the contact, and that Doc had taken care of the problem. They had barely moved twenty yards when Buck froze in place, then slowly lowered himself to the ground. Those behind him did the same. Novak slid up beside Buck. "What have we got, Buck?"

"The whole fuckin' North Vietnamese army."

Novak eased himself up on his elbows and peeked over the dead tree that he was lying behind. Buck wasn't exaggerating. Scattered before them were over one hundred NVA regulars dressed in khaki uniforms and pith helmets. A young NVA officer was going down the line issuing orders to his squad leaders. Novak's Vietnamese wasn't all that great, but he managed to catch a few of the words. Lowering himself back to the ground, he whispered, "They're supposed to stay out of sight until they get some kind of signal. He told them what it was, but I couldn't understand it. He was too far away."

"Okay, come on. We're gettin' the hell away from here. They must have over a company out there."

"At least that many," said Novak. "We need to let Stryker know."

"Okay, but not until we get far enough back so these boys can't pick up on it. Let's move."

Buck pulled back fifty yards before calling Stryker. Novak grabbed Buck's hand before he could key the switch. "Someone's coming," he whispered.

Merrill crawled up next to Buck. "We've got eight bandits coming up the draw and heading for the slope."

Buchanan looked toward the draw, then back to where the NVA were gathered. For a moment he considered taking down the bandits, but decided it was too risky. "Get our people under cover. We can't afford to start no shit with those NVA at our back door. Let the bandits pass."

Lobo Two went to ground and watched the eight men of Bao's advance patrol make their way to the base of the mountain. Buck and Novak had expected to see a reunion of NVA and bandits. What they got instead came as a total surprise. A group of twenty NVA suddenly swarmed out of the jungle and, leaping on the bandits, stabbed them to death. Novak cast a questioning glance at Buck, who seemed just as confused. Buck whispered, "What the hell is goin' on out here?"

They watched the NVA drag the bodies into the jungle and cover them up before fading back to where the NVA company was located. Moving the team father back, Buck called Stryker, "Lobo One Alpha, this is Lobo Two, over."

Stryker covered the radio in his hand. One of the NVA in front of them turned to stare in the team's direction. He thought he had heard something, and he was looking straight at Stryker's position. The NVA soldier began slowly walking toward the origin of the sound. Stryker eased the selector switch on his rifle to auto. The man was less than twenty feet away when an NVA officer called to the soldier to rejoin the group. Stryker breathed a sigh of relief as the soldier stared into the brush for a second, then turned and went back to join the mass of NVA troops that were forming up at the base of the slope. Stryker estimated at least a company of NVA regulars were in front of them. Moving back a few yards, he answered Buck's radio call. "Lobo Two, Lobo One Alpha. Go."

"One, this is Two. We got a situation here. Close to a hundred NVA regulars to our front. They're under orders to hold until they get some kind of signal. Till then, they're to stay out of sight. Over."

"Roger, Two. We got the same here on the west side. Over."

"One, this is Two. Be advised, we had eight bogeys come through here a few minutes ago, and these NVA whacked the shit out of 'em. Any idea what that's about? Over," whispered Buck.

Stryker paused a moment as he tried to think.

Doc had taken down seven bandits on the left, and now the NVA had dumped eight more on the right. Obviously, advance patrols sent out to recon before Bao and the main body showed up with the women. Bao didn't trust his Communist brothers, and with good reason. Those so-called brothers were planning to wipe out brother Bao and his army before the day was over. Caught in the middle of this mess were four innocent women and twenty American soldiers of fortune who should be back at Fort Bragg partying their asses off. But that wasn't the case. They were here and it was a situation that was going to have to be dealt with.

"Buck, for some reason the NVA have decided they don't want to play with brother Bao anymore. I believe they're going to try to get the women before they take Bao and the boys out, over."

"Sure seems that way, boss. Do we try to grab the women before the swap or after?" asked Buck.

This thing was getting complicated. Stryker only had twenty men. Bao had at least three hundred. The NVA had two companies that they had spotted already, and who was to say there weren't more to the north and south. As it stood now, Stryker could put his small force up against three hundred bandits or two hundred, and possibly more NVA regulars. Some choice! God, how he wished Jake had made it, but it was too late to think about that. He had to make a decision, and he had to make it now. If he were right, his best chance to grab the women would be during the confusion of the firefight between the NVA and the bandits. Best chance, hell! His only chance.

"Buck, we'll go after the trade. Once we have

the women, rally everyone in the rock formations on the south end of the plain. You copy? Over.''

''Roger, we're moving into position. Lobo Two, out.''

Bao's continuous calls to his patrols had only brought a reply from the one to the north. Where were the other two? He would have their heads when this was over. ''Phong! Bring those bitches up here.''

Phong pulled Maria to her feet and said, ''The nightmare is almost over for you all. I am certain that the government of Laos will return you to your embassy.''

Phong's reassuring words were a comfort to the women.

''Phong,'' barked Bao, ''you and I will escort the women to the meeting place. We will take ten of our men with us. The rest shall position themselves at the edge of the clearings to the east, north, and west.'' Bao paused. Maria was still holding Phong's hand tightly. ''That is, of course, if you think you can leave your new love long enough to carry out that order.''

Phong's eyes narrowed as he stared hard at Bao. Releasing Maria's hand, he never bothered to answer. He smiled at Maria and Denise, then left to coordinate the move.

Chapter 14

Stryker set the frequency on the PRC-70 radio and pressed the mike. "Wolf Pack, Wolf Pack, this is Lobo One, over." There was a pause, then Richards's voice came over the radio. "Lobo One, this is Wolf Pack, over."

Doc Shannon moved up next to Stryker before he answered the call, "Paul, we got a convoy coming up on the southwest end of the plain, four trucks and a jeep. Three of the trucks are covered, one is open and carrying troops."

Richards was still calling. "Lobo One, Lobo One, this is Wolf Pack, over."

"Get the people ready, Doc. This thing's going to go down quick when it starts," said Stryker as he pressed the mike.

"Wolf Pack, Lobo One. Get Eagle Wing warmed up. The show's about to begin. Tell Mitch we're going to be on the south end . . . I say again, the south end of the plain, not the north as we had planned. We now have a minimum of two NVA companies involved. The NVA are planning to give our boy Bao the short end of the stick on this deal. Should get damn interesting around here pretty quick. You copy? Over."

Bacher had already raced out of the room to

scramble the crews for their helicopters. Richards looked across the room at the stunned faces of Randolph and Edward Burford. First bandits and now North Vietnamese regulars. On the surface it seemed impossible odds, but these were men who were accustomed to bucking the odds and taking on the impossible.

"Lobo One, Wolf Pack, understand. Our friend with one eye has made some complimentary improvements on Eagle Wing's armament. We have added addition racks for more rockets, and Rick came up with a couple of mini-guns for the doors. Hope it will help, over."

"Can't hurt, Wolf Pack. We'll give you a call once the show starts. Do we still have an ETA of thirty minutes on Eagle Wing after launch request? Over."

"Roger, One. The additional weight will not affect their flight time, over."

"Roger Dodger, Wolf Pack." Stryker paused a moment, then added, "Mr. Randolph, sir, if this doesn't work out right, at least we tried. Lobo One, out."

Bao stood at the edge of the clearing with Phong, the women, and his ten-man squad. They watched in silence as the convoy made its way across the open center of the plain. Looking behind him, Bao saw that his men were beginning to deploy as per Phong's orders. The convoy was brought to a halt in the center of the clearing. Bao studied the distance of open ground between where he now stood and where the convoy had stopped. He estimated it to be 800 yards, a distance he was not entirely happy with, but then there were Diem, the Russian, and Major Thieu sitting clearly in the open. A white flag waved in the breeze above the jeep. Only 800 yards away was the gold that would provide for Bao's new life. It was time to go.

Five of the bandits moved out into the open in front of their leader. Bao and the women followed while Phong and the remaining five bandits brought up the rear of the line.

Diem and Kloskov stepped from the jeep. The wheels of destiny were now in motion. Both officers unsnapped the flaps of their holsters. Thieu stood on the far side of the jeep. A 12-gauge shotgun lay on the hood within easy reach. Twelve NVA troops dismounted the truck they were riding in and formed a semicircle around the three officers, their AK-47s set on full automatic.

Stryker and Shannon watched Bao emerge from the trees and walk to the center of the clearing. Stryker brought his field glasses up and sighted in on the blond woman directly behind Bao. It was Denise Randolph, behind her the three nuns. They looked a little rough and worn, but in remarkably good shape considering their situation. Buck lay on the edge of the clearing, across the way, and was doing the same thing as Stryker: staring through his binos at the four women. He hoped the older sisters could run fast enough to keep up when the shit hit the fan.

Bao stopped twenty yards short of the jeep.

"Colonel Diem, I wish you to move your men farther back. I shall leave my men an equal distance away as well."

Diem motioned to Thieu. The major waved the troops back.

"Does that meet with your approval, Colonel?"

Bao smiled a toothy grin as he nodded his approval, and began to move forward again. Phong stepped next to Maria and whispered, "Tell the sisters if there is any firing to drop down on the ground and not to move." Maria nodded that she understood and whispered the message to the others.

Bao stopped in front of the jeep. "As you can see, Comrades, the American women are fine. I had to give up much to get them back from their captors. I hope you have brought all that I asked for."

Kloskov was amazed that this arrogant bastard was still going through the motions of his earlier lie. Pulling the seal from the metal box on the hood, he opened the lid. The bright yellow of the gold sparkled in the morning sunlight. Two NVA soldiers left the circle and walked to the trucks, pulling back the canvas covers and revealing the weapons and ammunition that were stacked high in each of the trucks.

"Now," said Kloskov, "you will do as agreed and turn over the women."

"But of course, Colonel." Bao smiled. "I, too, am an honorable man. Phong! You will escort the women to the jeep, please."

Stryker keyed his team radio.

"Get ready, Buck. It's going down."

"Roger," acknowledged Buchanan.

Reaching for the long-distance radio, Stryker keyed the handset and spoke only three words, "Launch Eagle Wing."

Randy York rushed out the door and jumped into Bacher's chopper.

"Hit it, Mitch. We're on!"

Bacher raised his thumb as he revved the helicopter to maximum for liftoff. The other two choppers did the same. In less than a minute Eagle Wing was airborne. York stepped to the right door and double-checked the feed belt going to the mounted M-60 machine gun. Placing the headphones over his ears, he was greeted by the loud, hard-driving music of the Rolling Stones performing the song "I Can't Get No Satisfaction."

Phong helped the women into the jeep. Holding Maria's hand, he said, "It is most regrettable that our meeting should come under such circumstances. There is much I feel we could talk about. God go with you, Sister."

Maria squeezed his hand gently. Her eyes said more than she ever could. Denise reached over and gave him a kiss on the cheek. Smiling, she spoke in her little-girl voice, "Thank you, Phong, for everything."

Almost blushing, Phong released Maria's hand and walked back to stand next to Bao, who ordered two of his men to remove the gold from the jeep and take it back down the hill. Three more bandits moved to the loaded trucks and, pulling themselves up and behind the wheels of the big vehicles, they awaited orders to move out. Major Thieu was to take the jeep and the women back to the NVA troops so they would be out of the line of fire. Kloskov would give the signal to fire after the major brought the jeep back to pick up the colonels. That had been the plan, but as Thieu moved around to the driver's side of the vehicle, Bao said, "Major Thieu, the other day you were willing to risk death to look upon that blond-headed woman. What is the matter now? She has too many clothes on, perhaps.''

Thieu stopped and turned to face Bao. The shotgun hung loosely in the young major's hand. "You have your thieves' money, Bao. I would not push this matter any farther if I were you," said Thieu.

There was a strange silence around the group as Bao grinned; he loved it when he knew he was irritating the NVA officer. Elbowing Phong, who was standing next to him, Bao laughed. "Maybe he prefers to fuck the older one because it reminds him of his mother."

Kloskov saw the fire in Thieu's eyes and knew what was going to happen, but there was no time for him to react.

Major Thieu swung the shotgun up. Screaming, "You bastard," he fired. Bao and Phong dove out of the line of fire. The shotgun blast hit one of the men carrying the gold. The box fell to the ground, the gold bars spilling out onto the ground. Diem and Kloskov drew their pistols. Bao already had his out. Firing from the ground, he hit both officers. One round knocked Diem back against the hood of the jeep. The women screamed and huddled together in the seats. Phong, cussing Bao, and out of self-preservation, fired two slugs into Diem as he watched Kloskov recoil as Bao fired a round through the Russian's shoulder. Kloskov got off three shots as he was falling. Two hit Bao, one in the leg and the other in the chest. Phong fired at Kloskov; two bullets ripped through the Russian's midsection, driving him into the dirt.

The gunfire in the center of the clearing set off a wild flurry of firefights all around the plain as the NVA and the bandits unleashed their total firepower against each other. It was the confusion that Stryker had hoped for. The two opposing factions around the women were wiping each other out. Stryker saw a bandit trying to get the women out of the jeep and to cover behind the trucks. Bullets were kicking at the dirt around their feet. Pressing his mike, Stryker yelled, "Go for it, Buck. Good luck. See you on the south end. Out."

Buck and Novak led their team out of the trees and onto the eastern side of the clearing. They were cutting down NVA soldiers and bandits as they fought their way to the trucks.

Stryker and Doc broke out from the west side and began running as hard as they could for the same objective: the trucks and cover. The sounds of automatic weapons fire and grenade explosions rocked the normal peace of the Plain of Jars. Three bandits broke into the open on Stryker's left. Doc hit the ground, rolled over and took them out with three short bursts. Back on his feet, he caught up with Stryker. They were still 200 yards from the trucks. Across the plain they could see Buck and his group gaining ground among the confusion. Someone yelled out in pain behind Stryker. Glancing back, he saw one of Richards's men go down. A hole was in the side of his head. They knew they couldn't stop. They had to find cover, and the only available cover was the trucks.

Novak was breathing hard as they approached the remainder of Diem's escort. Bullets inched their way toward him as he calmly knelt down to squeeze off three quick shots which killed two NVA who pointed their weapons in Buck's direction. Two NVA on the western edge of the clearing stood and waved to the bandits, screaming for them to stop firing and pointing to the Americans rushing across the open ground. The bandits ignored them and, leveling their weapons at the two men, ripped them apart with a steady burst of automatic fire. Somewhere to his right, Buck heard the dull thud of bullets impacting with flesh and bone. He turned in time to see two of his men crumple into the dirt. They were both dead.

A hundred yards to go. Bullets were hitting around both teams like ice in a hailstorm. Buchanan felt a sharp pain rip through his right arm. Another bullet burned its way along his left side. He didn't stop moving. He tried to ignore the pain and kept on running.

Suddenly, a familiar voice cried out his name. It was Pete Merrill. He was down, and hit bad. Novak came up behind Merrill and dropped down beside the wounded man. Struggling, he got Merrill to his feet, only to have another bullet slam into the middle of Merrill's back. The impact knocked the man out of Novak's arms and facefirst into the dirt. Pete was dead before he hit the ground.

"Leave him, Novak!" screamed Buck.

Novak grabbed up his rifle and began to run again. He had made less than six steps before a round caught him just below the hip and spun him around. He hit the ground hard. His rifle flew out of his hands. The pain was unbelievable. He tried to get to his feet, but couldn't. Raising himself up on his forearms, he tried again. A second bullet tore through his left shoulder, slamming him back to the ground unconscious.

The NVA regulars were overcoming the bandits quickly. A few of the luckier bandits had thrown their weapons down as they ran away, leaving their comrades to face the wrath of the Vietnamese troops. Just as they had promised Kloskov, they were not taking any prisoners.

Phong pulled the women from the jeep and sheltered them behind one of the trucks. He quickly realized that this could be as hazardous as leaving them in the open because the truck they were behind was loaded with ammunition, but he had little choice. Phong moved to the rear of the truck and peered around the end as he tried to figure out who was shooting at whom. There were two groups of men running toward the trucks. One group was coming from the left, and the other was coming from the center of the clearing. They wore uniforms, but they were not NVA. They were being fired on by both the bandits and the Vietnamese. If he didn't know better, he'd swear they were Americans. Maria screamed, "Phong, look out!"

Phong turned just as Major Thieu, who had hidden under the jeep, fired a round from the shotgun. The bulk of the blast tore apart the hood of the truck. The remainder cut through Phong's right arm, shattering the elbow. Phong slumped back against the ruck, teetering on the verge of unconsciousness from the excruciating pain of the useless limb. His pistol lay at his feet. Thieu smiled broadly as he crawled out from under the jeep, and pumping another round into the shotgun, moved towards the wounded man.

"Now you will join your bastard leader in hell," he said.

Phong fought to focus his eyes for one last look at Maria.

Thieu raised the shotgun and pointed it at Phong's head. Three rapid shots rang out as Thieu pitched facefirst into the dirt. The three shots nearly cut the man's head off at the neck. Colonel Bao sat on the ground. A spreading red stain had appeared on the right side of his chest and his blood-soaked leg extended outward. His gun hung loosely in his hand as he lowered his head onto the bumper of the jeep. Killing Thieu had drained what little strength he had left. Maria and Sister Monica rushed to Phong's aid. Dragging him back behind the huge tires of the truck, Denise tore away a part of her shirt and handed it to Maria to stop the bleeding of the shattered arm.

"I . . . should have took you . . . that first day, bitch."

Denise looked up from Phong to see Bao staring at her. His pistol was pointed at her face as he continued. "But . . . no other shall have you either."

"No!" yelled Sister Monica as she pushed Denise out of the way just as Bao fired. The bullet hit the nun between the eyes. Denise screamed as Monica's blood splattered her face and clothes.

Through blurring eyes, Bao swung the pistol back in Denise's direction, but before he could fire two bullets struck him in the back. One severed his spine. Blood poured from his mouth as he slumped against the bumper of the jeep. His now empty hand twitched twice before he died. Denise lowered her hands from her blood-covered face in time to see Colonel Kloskov force a labored smile at her before lowering his head to the ground. His pistol dropped from his lifeless hand. Bao had been right all along; the Russian had saved her.

"Denise! Denise! Get Bao's gun. Hurry, Denise!" yelled Maria.

The young girl was still in shock but did as Maria said. Grabbing the weapon, she moved back to Maria's side. Sister Helen covered Sister Monica's face as she knelt down to pray over her friend's body. Phong lost consciousness as Maria held his head in her lap. Denise huddled close to her. Would the nightmare never end?

A loud clamor of automatic weapons fire erupted from the other side of the vehicle as something banged against the truck. A body came rolling over the hood and hit haphazardly in a pile before the terrified women. Denise pointed the gun at the figure and fired wildly. The bullets threw dirt into the air only inches from the man's head.

"Holy shit, lady! I'm on your side," screamed Stryker.

The women stared with disbelief at the camouflaged face of the American soldier of fortune. Their disbelief went from one of shock to screams of tearful joy. Someone was here to save them. They hadn't been forgotten.

Doc Shannon dove around the corner of the truck as a hail of bullets tore up the ground only inches from his heels.

"Goddamn dildoheads!" he shouted as he pulled himself up, wiping dirt from his mouth. Looking up, he saw the kindly face of Sister Helen. He apologized. "Oh . . . I'm . . . I'm sorry, Sister. I . . ."

"No need, my son. Your choice of terminology was much kinder than what I was thinking of those assholes. Are you all right?"

Shannon nodded that he was, and smiled. The smile quickly vanished when he spotted the body of Sister Monica. He moved to check her out. Sister Helen raised her hand to stop him. In a motherly voice she said, "She is beyond help, my son, but if you could please look after this man's arm." She pointed to Phong.

"But Sister, he is one of them."

"He is our friend. Please."

Stryker was on his feet now, looking over the hood of the truck and trying to locate Buck and Lobo Two. He asked, "Doc! How many of our guys made it?"

Shannon continued to work on Phong as he glanced back at the second truck and made a quick count. "Six, counting us. How about Buck?"

"I don't know, I'm . . . Wait! There they are. Novak's down. Buck's trying to get him up, and the rest of the team are covering him."

A group of five NVA were rushing up on Buck's blind side. The team didn't see them coming. Stryker lowered the barrel of his rifle onto the hood and, switching to semiautomatic fire, pulled off five rapid shots. Three found their mark and tumbled three of the NVA, but the other two went wide. Sighting in on them, Stryker squeezed the trigger. *Click*—he was out of ammo.

Buck dropped Novak and swung his rifle up, firing the last five rounds of his magazine into one of the men. The second NVA was also out of ammo and swung the butt of his AK at Buchanan's head. Buck dodged the blow and brought his knee up into the man's groin, then butt-stroked him backwards with the end of his rifle. Buck screamed for the rest of the team to make a break for the trucks. They looked back at him, concerned about leaving their leader and Novak. "Get the fuck outta here! That's an order." They did as they were told and broke for the trucks. Releasing the empty magazine, Buck grabbed for another when three more NVA came charging straight at him. There wasn't time to reload. From somewhere near the trucks came two shots that took one of the NVA down. Buck threw his rifle at one of the men, knocking him down, and grabbing the third by the front of his shirt, fell backwards and at the same time planted his boot in the man's stomach and flipped him end over end. Pulling the knife from his web gear, he leaped on top of the stunned man and drove his knife through the NVA's chest.

"Look out!" screamed Novak.

Before Buck could react, he felt a sharp pain enter his side and pierce his body. The NVA soldier's bayonet had gone straight through him, the tip protruding out of Buchanan's back, just below the shoulder blade. Novak managed to raise his pistol and shoot the man twice before another NVA rushed up and placed the barrel of his rifle against the ex-Marine's head and pulled the trigger. Novak's head exploded like a busted water balloon. Buck tried to get up, but staggered and fell.

"Doc! Buck's down!" yelled Stryker. "You take our four guys and the women and get to the rocks on the south end. I'm going after Buck. If I don't make it, you get the people out of here. Move it, Doc!"

Stryker slammed home a fresh magazine and broke into a dead run for Buck and Novak. Two bandits came up on his right. He let loose a short burst that dropped them both. Buck was still moving. He wasn't dead. The NVA who had killed Novak now turned toward Buck. Two of Buck's team looked back and saw what was happening. They stopped, turned and, kneeling, fired at the same time, killing the man before he could fire at their leader on the ground. However, their pause to save Buck proved fatal; both men were caught in the crossfire between bandits and NVA. Bullets were hitting all around Stryker as he dove into the dirt next to Buck. Rolling the big man over, he saw the stream of blood that was streaming down the side of his mouth.

"Buck! Godamn you, Buck! Don't you die on my ass. You hear me?"

Buchanan opened his tired eyes and forced a smile across his pain-racked face. A trickle of blood began to leak from his nose and made its way down the corner of his mouth to his chin.

"How . . . how you doing, boss? Guess we . . . we just had too . . . too many Indians 'round us . . . this time."

"You're gonna be fine, Buck. Mitch will be here any minute with the choppers and we'll be outta here. You just hang on, partner."

Buck coughed a deep painful cough, then asked, "Did we . . . did we get the ladies away . . . away from the bad guys, boss?"

Stryker's eyes were filling with tears as he looked down into the face of the man who was like a brother to him.

"Yeah . . . yeah, Buck, we got 'em back."

Buck smiled again.

"Knew . . . knew we could do it. You . . . tell Sharon . . . she ever gets tired . . . of your . . . your old ragged ass . . . Ol' Bucky . . . will . . . ."

Stryker could not control the flood of emotion that poured from his very soul as Buck's words faded. "Oh God! No! Oh, Buck, I'm so sorry."

Stryker cradled the man in his arms and, pulling him to his chest, he cried. Buck was dead.

Two members of Lobo Two had doubled back and were screaming at Stryker. "Stryker! Stryker, come on, man! We have to go. Leave him, he's dead. Let's go! The whole fucking NVA army is massing on the north end."

Stryker wiped the tears from his eyes. Removing the rag from around Buck's neck, he unfolded it and placed it over his friend's face. Squeezing Buck's hand in a final good-bye, he quickly turned to check Novak. Half the man's head was gone. He had fought like a true Marine to the very end. Jumping to his feet, Stryker looked down at Buck one last time, then yelled, "Let's go!" All three men made a mad dash toward the cover of the vehicles.

Shannon started a truck and placed the women and his four men on the side. He moved the truck slowly but surely for the rocks. Bullets clanked and pinged into the hood and the doors, two of the tires were blown out, but Doc kept the truck moving. It was their only chance. Major Phong had been placed on the running board.

Stryker and the two remaining members of Lobo Two threw themselves behind the jeep as a rain of lead ripped into the metal frame. Catching his breath, one of the men asked, "Where in the hell are those choppers?"

"They'll be here. You can count on it. Come on, let's try Doc's tactic," said Stryker as he reached into the jeep, flipped the switch on, and keeping as low as possible, slid into the driver's seat. Starting the engine, he began to inch the jeep forward with the two men moving slowly along the side and providing what little cover fire they could. A round made its way through the metal and struck Stryker in the leg. His foot slipped off the clutch, and the jeep jerked forward to a stop. A second bullet cut a groove across Stryker's back. The burning sensation was almost unbearable. Stryker threw himself out of the jeep and onto the ground just as a burst of automatic weapons fire tore the front seat to shreds. This was as far as they were going.

Stryker fought back the pain that was coursing through his body. Releasing an empty magazine from his rifle, he pushed a new one into place. The remaining bandits around the plain were being systematically wiped out by mop-up squads of NVA. The bulk of the force was now concentrating its attention on the Americans. Stryker noticed the wide-eyed look his wounds were getting from one of the young men. The boy was scared, there was little doubt about that.

"What's your name, kid?"

"Rogan. Mike Rogan, Sergeant Stryker."

Glancing at the other trooper, he asked, "And you. What's your name, son?"

"Jeff Dahlby, Sarge."

"Sorry, fellows. I usually make it a habit to know the names of my men, but this whole business has been kind of a rushed affair. Now, I don't want you two to worry about anything. Old One-Eye will be coming over that ridge line any minute now. Then you're going to get to see something you can tell your grandkids about. Okay?"

Dahlby and Rogan looked at each other, then back to Stryker. It was kind of hard to take seriously reassurance from somebody who was bleeding all over the place. But, then, Stryker was supposed to be the best in the business. They nodded and tried to relax.

Doc had made it to the rocks. The truck was a burning hulk. A lucky round had hit the gas tank only minutes after the survivors had reached the rocks. Stryker had thought of trying to make a run for it, but the rocks were still over a hundred yards away. They wouldn't have a chance. Nearly ninety NVA had massed at the north end of the clearing and another fifty were regrouping to the west. Stryker couldn't tell how many were to the east. Counting himself, Stryker had only nine men left.

Dahlby heard it first. Although it was still a ways off, it was definitely the sound of helicopters. Rogan smiled as he heard the sound.

"Damn, Top! You called it. Here they come."

Pulling the radio from his web gear, Stryker began the call. "Eagle Wing, this is Lobo One. Get your ass in here. We got the women and the pimps are mad as hell."

Bacher's voice hinted of zealous excitement as he replied, "You hang in there, Home-Boy. We're coming in with our ass on fire and daring anybody to fuck with us."

"I got troops massing on the west, east, and north. Doc's got the people in the rocks to the south and we're pinned down behind the jeep in the center of the clearing—say again, friendlies behind the jeep and in the rocks to the south."

"Roger . . . uh . . . uh, shit! I forgot the damn call sign. Hell, Stryker, I got ya. Keep your heads down till we dust these boys a few times. Out."

The three choppers broke the horizon and zoomed across the open plain. Bacher, in the lead ship, banked hard left, moving toward the trees along the northern slope. The mini-gun roared, sounding more like a long, loud belch than a deadly weapon that could rain down 6,000 rounds of death per minute.

The Eagle Two bird banked right to take on the troops to the west. Eagle Three went east. The traffic coming over the radio was hot and heavy as the gun runs were made and repeated.

"Eagle One, you caught 'em with their dick skinners down, ol' buddy," yelled Big Tit Tillman.

"Hot damn, Mitch, I got twenty in the open. Goin' for it," said Shanassey.

Dave Rowe pulled out of a gun run just in time to see three NVA making their way up to the edge of the slope. He yelled in a panic, "Watch your asses. Got three bad guys on the west with a fuckin' Stinger!"

The word *Stinger* brought a sudden stop to all the bullshit on the radios. Bacher's voice was cool and collected as he asked, "Eagle Three, give me a definite location on that heat-seeker missile team."

"At your two o'clock, just beyond the lip of the ridge. Over."

"I got it—break, Eagle Two you go down for the extraction. Eagle Three, you'll fly cover. I'm going for the Stinger! One out."

Bacher banked the UH1H around and headed straight at the position Rowe had called in. He was less than a hundred feet off the ground. He was moving fast as he passed over Stryker's location. The three men behind the jeep had monitored the conversation on the radio.

"Jesus, Stryker, he's going right at them," said Rogan.

"You got it, kid. Mitch Bacher doesn't fuck around. He'll keep it low, zigzag her a few times to throw those boys off, then he'll be on top of 'em before they know what happened."

Bacher tilted the stick left, then right, and back left again. Big Mo' Morano slowly raised his sunglasses, allowing them to rest on the top of the bright orange sweatband he wore that read SOMETIMES LIFE'S A BITCH. Small beads of sweat began to appear at the corners of Morano's lips. If Bacher missed on the first pass, they could kiss their asses good-bye. Behind them sat York and J. J. Johnson. They were still firing at targets of opportunity that came up on either side of them.

As they sped across the center of the clearing, York stopped firing and leaned out, looking back behind the chopper, reconfirming what he had thought he had seen. There were four American bodies on the ground back there. One of them had been Buck Buchanan. Pressing his throat mike, York said, "Mitch! That was—"

Bacher cut him off. "I know, Major—not now, please, I'm kinda busy up here."

Moran began the countdown, "Fifteen seconds . . . ten . . . five . . . Now!"

Bacher hauled back on the stick, kicking his left foot on the rudder, and practically stood the bird on its tail as he banked hard, coming back directly over and behind the startled trio of NVA.

"Surprise, motherfuckers! Ya thought I'd fly by and let you burn that missile right up my ass, didn't ya? Well, you lose, sweetheart."

Bacher thumbed the trigger and four 3.7 rockets

snaked their way into the middle of the Stinger team. The explosion of the rockets and the Stinger missile sent dirt, rock, and body parts sailing through the sky in an ashen gray cloud.

Mark Shanassey swung Eagle Two in low over the rocks to the south. Hovering thirty feet overhead, he keyed his radio mike, ''Hey Doc, your taxi's here. But you better get a move on, the meter's runnin'.''

The women shielded their eyes from the dust and dirt that whirled around them. Shannon couldn't be heard over the heavy drone of the rotor blades. Reaching out, he grabbed Sister Helen by the arm and pulled her up on the rocks. Wrapping his arms around her buttocks, he yelled ''Sorry, Sister!'' as he lifted her up to the outstretched hands of Steve Graham, who was leaning out of the chopper as Shanassey began to lower the bird. Grabbing her wrists, he pulled the nun up and into the chopper.

Stryker watched as the woman was pulled into the helicopter. A sense of accomplishment swept over him. At the same moment, there was the painful knowledge of what it had cost. Two bullets ricocheted off the side of the jeep, reminding Stryker that they weren't out of this thing yet.

Eagle Three was making a gun run to cover the extraction when Bacher came up on the radio. ''Hey, old man! You gonna lie behind that piece of shit jeep and play with yourself all day or what?''

Rogan and Dahlby shook their heads in wonder. None of the old guys seemed to be taking any of this very seriously.

Stryker grinned as he keyed his radio and said, ''If I could get some damn cover fire from one of you hot dogs up there, we might be able to make it to the extraction point before the sun goes down, you one-eyed fuck!''

"Baby, you want cover fire—you got it. Just tell me when.''

Stryker motioned for Rogan and Dahlby to get ready to make a run for it. They both looked down at his blood-soaked pants leg. Stryker said, "Hey, you two just go when I tell you to. Don't worry about me. I'll get there. Now get ready. Okay, Mitch, action talks and bullshit walks! Let's do it.''

"You got it, Paul. Go on my command . . . break . . . break, Eagle Three, line up across from me on this run. We're going to give our boys an alley to run through.'' Bacher waited until Rowe had brought his chopper around, then said, "Okay, Three, bank it now. Hit it! Go Stryker!''

The three men were up and moving. Rogan and Dahlby cut left, then right as they made their way to the rocks. Stryker was half hopping, half dragging his wounded leg. He was falling farther behind. Dahlby looked back, but Stryker waved for him to keep going.

Eagles One and Three were tearing up the ground along the east and west slopes with rockets and machine gun fire. They were trying their best to keep the NVA heads down, but small puffs of dirt still popped up around the three men. Rogan and Dahlby made it to the rocks. Stryker was still twenty yards short of the rocks when he was hit again. The bullet struck him in the right arm, just below the elbow, breaking the bone and spinning him to the ground. Stryker lay on his back staring up at the clouds. They weren't white clouds. They seemed to be flashing bright orange, then fire red.

He felt himself slipping away as the pain sent shock wave after shock wave through his exhausted body.

Doc had just pulled Maria up onto the rocks when he saw Stryker go down. At the same instant, two bullets punched their way through the Plexiglas of Mark Shanassey's helicopter. One struck him square in the chest and drove him back in the seat. The second ripped through his side. His eyes focused on the two small holes in the glass as he spit blood and uttered, "Now . . . ain't that . . . some shit." Then died.

The chopper lifted suddenly, then teetered to the left. Donny Shanassey grabbed for the controls and fought to level the bird out. It was too late. The chopper rose seventy-five feet, tilting wildly to the left. It spilled Sister Helen and Steve Graham out the side door and to their deaths on the rocks below. The chopper then rolled completely over and crashed into the ground. A bright red-orange fireball rose in the sky as it exploded.

"My God, Mitch, they got Mark." The statement from Eagle Three came in a stunned whisper.

There was a long silence before Bacher replied. "Eagle Three, you are now the extraction bird. I will fly cover. Let's move it. One out."

Dave Rowe brought Eagle Three around, coming in low from the south. As they passed over the trees of the southern slopes, they were met by a sheet of automatic weapons fire. Hartman, the door gunner, was knocked backwards from his machine gun. With three holes through his abdomen, he hit the steel floor unconscious.

Bud Tillman unhooked himself from the co-pilot's seat and climbed between the seats to go back to Hartman's aid. His feet slipped on the steel floor and he suddenly realized that hydraulic fluid was leaking from a shattered line. It snapped the rest of the way and began to spray the cabin like a broken water sprinkler.

"Rowe! We're hit! Losing hydro and heating up fast," yelled Tillman.

Rowe radioed Bacher. "Mitch! Mitch! We're in trouble—took a hit in the hydraulics, over."

"Break off, Eagle Three, and head back to base. Good luck. Eagle One, out."

"You too, Mitch. You, too. Three out."

Stryker opened his eyes just as Eagle Three passed over them, trailing a line of smoke behind its engine. Dahlby and Rogan had braved the small arms fire to bring Stryker into the rocks. A pretty blond girl with soft teary blue eyes was trying to bandage his broken arm.

"You must be Denise Randolph."

"Yes, Sergeant Stryker, I am."

Doc came over and knelt beside him. "How you doing, Paul?"

"I've felt a lot better, Doc. Are we winning or losing?"

Doc didn't have to say anything; Stryker could see the sadness in the medic's eyes as he said, "We've lost Eagle Two, all dead. Eagle Three was hit and had to return to base. Mitch is trying to hold them back with gun runs, but he can't have much fuel left. Sorry, Paul, but it doesn't look good."

The sound of AK rounds ricocheting off Eagle One echoed across the open plain. Stryker reached for his radio. Blinding pain shot through his damaged arm. Denise leaned forward and unhooked the small radio, placing it in his good hand.

"Mitch, this is Paul. Break it off, buddy. You've done all you can. We gave it a shot and just came up a little short. Happens to the best of 'em. I know you're running low on fuel, so get your lovely, one-eyed ass out of here. You copy? Over."

Bacher wanted to scream at the world. Not because of what his friend had said, but because he was right. The fuel gauges were dropping fast. They might not have enough to make it back, even if they left now. Bacher saw Morano looking at the gauges, too. Speaking softly into the throat mike, Bacher asked, "How we doing ammowise, you guys?"

"Maybe three hundred rounds," replied Johnson.

"I have even less," said York.

Bacher checked his weapons. He had one single rocket left. "What d' you want to do, Major York?" asked Mitch.

"How long for us to get to base, refuel, rearm, and get back here?"

"Ninety minutes, minimum."

York leaned forward and looked over the plain. Even with all the devastating gun runs they had made on the NVA, there were still close to a hundred men running around down there. Stryker and his small group couldn't hold out for an hour and a half against those odds. York asked, "Mitch, any chance of getting anyone out of there?"

Bacher wished he could say yes, but he couldn't. "Sir, I'll be honest with you. Without someone to run cover for us, we wouldn't last thirty seconds down there if we tried to hover for a pickup. Stryker knows that. That's why he's telling us to bug out."

York keyed his radio. "Stryker, this is York. We're going back to refuel and to reload. We'll be back. You've got to try and hold on. You copy?"

"Roger, sir. But I'd call in advance before you come back. Just to make sure we still own this piece of the rock."

Mitch swung the chopper around and fired his last rocket at the largest concentration of NVA at the northern slope.

"Hang tough, Paul. We'll be back, buddy, you got my word on that," said Bacher as he headed the helicopter for Nakhon Phanom.

The eight men and two women watched as the chopper became no more than a fading dot in a distant sky. A strange, almost eerie, silence fell over the Plain of Jars. To the north, the NVA were regrouping, joined now by the third company that had been held in reserve. They were preparing to make their move on the tiny rock fortress that contained the Americans. Stryker took a quick count of their ammunition situation. It wasn't much. Most of the claymores had been left with the rucksacks that had been dropped during the mad dash for the trucks. The supply of small arms ammo was desperately low. Not nearly enough to hold out for ninety minutes. The soldiers all knew that, but didn't want the women to worry anymore than they already were.

They didn't have to wait long. With the departure of the helicopter, the NVA walked boldly out into the open and began advancing toward the rocks. Long bayonets that had been swung out from under the barrels of Russian AK-50s glimmered in the morning sunlight. Stryker and the others knew that there would be no prisoners taken. They prepared, as best they could, to die, hoping only that they could extract a deadly price from their killers before the end came.

An NVA mortar squad set up a 60-mm in the clearing. *Thump*—the first round was on its way.

"Incoming!" screamed Doc, as everyone hugged the ground.

The round was short of its target, but it still shook the ground around them. Maria leaned over Phong in an effort to protect him from the rocks and dirt that rained down on them. Three more rounds were fired in rapid succession. One was long, one was short, but the third was close enough to blow Dahlby out from behind a small outcropping of rocks he had selected for cover.

Doc scrambled on his hands and knees to the man's side. Dahlby's ears were bleeding from the concussion, and there were multiple shrapnel wounds to his face and right chest area.

"How is he, Doc?" called Stryker.

"A little ventilated, but he'll be okay."

The sound of mortar rounds being fired had increased to an impossible rate. There were ten explosions in rapid succession, but none of the rounds had hit anywhere around the rock fortress.

"What the hell . . ." whispered Stryker, as he carefully raised his head and looked across the open ground. The NVA were rushing around like rats in a trap as round after round of mortar fire exploded in their midst, knocking them off their feet. Attempts to run back to the cover of the trees were met by a barrage of incoming rounds that walked a deadly path in front of them, cutting them off. As suddenly as it had started, it ended. The NVA slowly got to their feet. Their ranks had been thinned considerably. They had lost twenty killed by the mortar barrage. They milled around, unsure of what to do next and equally confused as to who had fired on them. One of the young NVA officers was screaming for someone to point out who had fired on them. Who?

The answer to the question came in the form of a low chanting sound that began to the east. The tempo increased as the chanting became louder and louder. It seemed to be coming from everywhere. The NVA soldiers were gathering around each other, forming a large circle in the middle of the plain. The chanting suddenly stopped. It was followed by a full thirty seconds of maddening silence. Then, one lone voice gave a high-pitched yell that seemed to roll like thunder across the vastness of the Plain of Jars.

The NVA were terrified. They had reason to be, for that one yell was followed by nearly a thousand more as the Meo tribesmen began to pour over the slopes from all sides. They had only one objective: the circle of hated North Vietnamese solders.

The stone fortress defenders all turned to Stryker with a questioning look. Stryker grinned as he shouted, "Those are all Jake McKenna's relatives. The son of a bitch is still alive!"

A wild cheer went up from the group as the tribesmen charged headlong into the NVA. It was over in a matter of minutes. There were no survivors among the North Vietnamese. Stripping the dead of their weapons and ammunition, all but a few of the Meo were already leaving the battlefield. A small contingent made its way to the rocks. Jake lay on a makeshift stretcher. Bamboo served as splints for his broken legs. Both of his eyes were black, and he had a nasty-looking cut running down the entire left side of his face. Stryker motioned his group out of the rocks to meet the Meo. Forgetting the pain of his wounds, Stryker smiled at Jake. "Damn good to see you, Jake. We thought you'd bought it."

"Would have if it hadn't been for these boys. They found me hanging from a tree out cold. Man, was I screwed up. Broke both legs. Guess I tried to move a tree with my face, too. Broke my nose and almost fileted half my face. Worst fuckin' exit I ever made from an aircraft in over twenty-three years."

"Rick Alley's boys reported seeing a body with the chute," said Doc Shannon.

"That was one of the guys from a Pathet Lao patrol. They were climbing up to get me when the Meo showed up. They killed them all and just left one of 'em in the trees. Just what the hell happened in that plane, Paul?" asked Jake.

"Anchor cable broke when you went out, Jake."

"Well, brother, that's it for this ol' boy. No more of this Rambo shit. I'm getting too old for it. Is this our Miss Randolph?" asked Jake, smiling at the dirty-faced blonde.

"That's her," said Stryker. "She's a pretty tough kid, too. Denise, this is Mr. Jake McKenna."

Denise came over and held Jake's hand.

"I'm very glad to meet you, Mr. McKenna. If you and . . . your family, I believe is what Sergeant Stryker called them, hadn't shown up—"

Jake interrupted as he said, "Hell, look at me! I been laid up a couple of days and done forgot my manners. Miss Randolph—boys, I'd like you to meet my adoptive father. This is King Muong Ti Sing, and your rescuers are his loyal subjects.''

Stryker bowed to the king. The others followed his lead as Jake asked, "Hey, where's Buck?"

Stryker looked out over the plain.

"Out there. Him, Novak, Merrill, and a lot of other good men."

Jake was sorry he had asked.

"What do you plan to do now, Paul?" asked Jake.

"Mitch Bacher's supposed to be coming back with a couple of choppers. If we're lucky, they're already on their way, but man, we haven't had a hell of a lot of luck on this mission.''

"More than you know, ol' buddy. Didn't you wonder why these NVA didn't have half the Laotian air force and army on your asses before this?" said Jake.

"Now that you mention it, we haven't seen anything but bandits and Vietnamese. And not one Laotian plane or chopper.''

"That's right. It's considered bad politics to go around knocking off the people who work for you. Makes everyone a little nervous. This was supposed to be a by-invitation-only party. Limited personnel were to be involved. Easier to hide it that way. They just hadn't figured on you boys showing up," said Jake.

"Well, I be damned, guess we were luckier than we thought."

Jake said something to the king, and he sent some of his men away. The whopping sounds of chopper blades could be heard in the far distance. Bacher's voice came over the radio to confirm that Stryker and his people were still alive. Alley had managed to come up with three more helicopters. They were five minutes out.

Stryker turned to Jake and asked, "Jake, do you think I could get the king to bring the bodies of—"

"Already taken care of, Paul. We're taking them all home."

McKenna spent a few minutes alone with his Meo father as the team, the women, and the bodies of the dead were loaded aboard the choppers. No one knew what was said, but there were tears in Jake's eyes as he was loaded aboard Eagle One. York was relaying the good news to an ecstatic headquarters. Denise would soon be reunited with her father. This time they would have a lot to talk about. Maria had told the group all that Major Phong had done to help them through their ordeal and that Denise intended to use her father's influence to take him back to the United States. She would see to it that the best surgeons money could buy would repair their friend's shattered arm. Jake wanted only to get back home. He knew he had been given a second chance by a higher power, and this time he wasn't going to blow it.

Stryker leaned back against the rear of the chopper pilot's seat. His eyes lingered on the brightly colored Meo blanket of red, black, and white stripes that covered Buck's body. There would never be another friend like him. They had shared so much together, the good times and the bad. There was an old saying that they had in Vietnam for the CCN recon teams: "You have never lived until you have almost died. Life has a special meaning that the protected will never know."

* * *

Bacher gave the word and the choppers lifted off. They circled over the plain of death one last time, then gained altitude as they headed back for Nakhon Phanom and the safety of Thailand.

Below, King Sing waved until the choppers were out of sight. Then, raising his arm, he turned and led his people back into the jungle. Their battle was not over. It would never be over until they had rid their country of the Pathet Lao and the North Vietnamese. He had asked Jake when the Americans would be coming back to honor the promises they had made to the Meo during the Vietnam War. The question had brought tears to the veteran Green Beret's eyes, for he knew Sing and his people had been abandoned by America. No longer was anyone interested in Southeast Asia or the suffering of its people. McKenna had no answer for his Meo father.

Doc Shannon had put Jake out with a healthy dose of morphine. Then he began to work on McKenna's broken legs. Randy York inched his way over to Stryker. "What'll you do now, Paul?"

"I don't know, Major. Take Buck back home first, then go see Sharon. I think it's about time I started thinking about settling down."

"Quit the business for good, huh, Paul?"

"Yeah. It just wouldn't be the same without Buck."

York glanced at the blanket-covered body as he said, "Yeah. I see your point. You guys did a hell of a job out there, Paul."

A frown etched its way across Stryker's brow. "Yeah, but it was damn expensive, Major."

York nodded in silence. He could sense that the big man didn't want to talk about it anymore. Quietly he went back to his seat and left Stryker to his thoughts of the future.

The reunion at NKP had been a mixed one of cheers, handshaking, back slapping, tears, and grief for those who had been lost. Richards handled the arrangements for the return of the bodies to the States. Bobby Joe and the others expressed their sorrow to Stryker over the loss of Buck Buchanan. Johnathan Randolph told Stryker that if he ever needed anything to never hesitate to call upon him. Maria and Denise hugged and kissed Stryker before they left. For them it was over. For Paul Stryker, it was not over until the day he stood in a light Texas rain and watched his best friend lowered to his final resting place. Then it was over.

Three months had passed since that sad day. He had returned to Sharon. They had been married one week later. Now, lying on the beach together, Sharon asked him about Jake.

"He's doing fine, honey. Got enough money to get himself straightened out and off the booze. Randolph kicked in a healthy bonus. Jake won't have to worry about working anymore. Charlotte's been calling him every week. She's supposed to be coming up next week to see him. I think they've got it worked out now."

"Oh, that's wonderful, Paul. Maybe we can all get together when she comes and go . . ." Sharon's voice trailed off as she stared down the beach at the two men walking toward them. It was Erin Richards and Randy York. The colonel was carrying a briefcase. By their manner of walking and the looks of seriousness in their faces she knew it was not just a friendly visit.

"Oh no, not again. . . ."